'Problems already?'

Leonie smiled. 'The answer is no,' she said lightly. 'At least none that you could help me with.'

Adam's face was lightening. 'That makes a change. Most people think I have a magic wand that will solve everything.'

'And who solves your problems, Adam?' she asked softly, aware that she was being a trifle familiar with the big chief of hospital management.

There was surprise in the dark eyes looking into hers. 'I put them up on the shelf and hope they'll go away,' he said drily.

Abigail Gordon is fascinated by words, and what better way to use them than in the crafting of romance between the sexes? A state of the heart that has affected almost everyone at some time of their lives. Twice widowed, she now lives alone in a Cheshire village. Her two eldest sons between them have presented her with three delightful grandchildren, and her youngest son lives nearby.

Recent titles by the same author:

SAVING FACES
DR BRIGHT'S EXPECTATIONS
POLICE SURGEON

FINGER ON
THE PULSE

BY
ABIGAIL GORDON

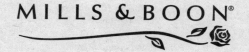

MILLS & BOON®

For Stephen, who knows what it's all about.

All the characters in this book have no existence outside the imagination of the author, and have no relation whatsoever to anyone bearing the same name or names. They are not even distantly inspired by any individual known or unknown to the author, and all the incidents are pure invention.

First published in Great Britain 2000
Harlequin Mills & Boon Limited,
Eton House, 18-24 Paradise Road, Richmond, Surrey TW9 1SR

© Abigail Gordon 2000

ISBN 0 263 82258 3

Set in Times Roman 10½ on 11½ pt.
03-0009-53496

Printed and bound in Spain
by Litografía Rosés, S.A., Barcelona

CHAPTER ONE

STRIDING briskly through Accident and Emergency, Adam Lockhart was immediately aware that the May bank holiday weekend had taken its toll. Every seat in the waiting area was taken.

As his thoughtful dark eyes, behind the sunglasses that he'd worn in the car, raked the room, years of experience and an instinct that was like radar when it came to hospital situations told him that there was unrest in the air.

If he'd needed confirmation, the muted smile of the receptionist, the distracted air of the triage nurse and the way the bushy mop of the registrar in charge was standing on end would have been enough.

But further proof was on hand in the form of a tubby, middle-aged man with a bloodied nose who, on observing the respectful greetings of the staff for the imposing figure in the smart business suit, bellowed, 'How much longer am I going to have to wait? There's more men in suits around the place than white coats. Too many chiefs and not enough Indians!'

Ignoring the outburst, Adam cast a wry smile in the direction of the young doctor in charge, and with a brief inclination of his head indicated that the registrar follow him into the corridor at the far end of the unit.

'What's wrong?' Adam asked. 'I know you're busy, but is that all?'

The registrar shook his head. 'No, not exactly, Mr Lockhart. There was a disturbance earlier. Some youths who'd been out all night, drinking, brought along a friend who'd been hurt in a fight and one of them assaulted a nurse.'

Adam frowned. It wasn't the first time one of his staff had been at risk and it wouldn't be the last, but it didn't make it any easier to accept that those who were trying to serve the sick and injured were sometimes hurt while doing so.

'Where is she now?' he asked with the crisp incisiveness that had taken him to the top rank of his profession.

'Resting in the staffroom. She wasn't hurt, but she's badly shaken and isn't fit to come back on duty.'

'So you need a replacement. Has the nursing manager been contacted?'

'Er…yes, but I don't think she's arrived. It was barely eight o'clock when it happened and she's been having trouble with her car.'

Adam sighed. If Joanne Archer didn't get herself some reliable transport soon he was going to…what? Lend her his? Hardly. But Joanne, a divorced mother of two, really did need to get her act together.

After he'd sent the young nurse home in a taxi Adam continued his progress to the office that saw more of his presence than *The Adam's Apple*, his picturesque houseboat, so named because of his affection for it rather than any other connotation.

Situated on a marina in a Cheshire village within motoring distance of Manchester, *The Apple* had proved to be an ideal residence when he'd found himself alone after losing Annabel.

Its peaceful surroundings were a pleasant contrast to the noise and bustle of the city, and on the rare occasions that he entertained, his guests were enthralled with the surroundings.

As he deposited his briefcase on the polished surface of his desk the words of the restive patient in Accident and Emergency came to mind.

He'd heard it all before. How there were too many administrators and not enough hands-on staff. It wasn't true, of course, but the press were always ready to make something out of nothing, given the chance.

With that thought came a vision of the empty soup can that was still gracing the drainer in his kitchen from the night before. It was all he'd felt like bothering with when he'd got home at ten o'clock after a particularly long meeting of the trust board.

But he supposed that it was only to be expected that the public saw the likes of himself as superfluous when it came to health care. They only cared about what was known in the business as 'the coal face'—the wards, the doctor with his stethoscope, the nurses, the scanning machines, X-ray units and suchlike.

The fact that those things were there, working and paid for, had to be due to someone—and he was that someone. Out of sight, in the background, but always with his finger on the pulse.

'Morning, Mr Lockhart.'

Jean Telfer, his secretary, was looming up with the mountain of paperwork that would be today's quota after she had painstakingly sifted out every possible item that she could deal with herself.

They were a good team. St Mark's Hospital, covering Manchester and the surrounding areas, was the centre of the no-nonsense, elderly spinster's life, and Adam supposed the same applied to himself. He certainly spent enough time on its affairs but, then, he had time to spare. Nobody else needed him.

His mother had left home when he was small, and his father, having been on his own for years, had recently taken a new wife and was now living an idyllic life in Kenya. His own wife, Annabel, had died three years previously, after contracting meningitis while they'd been on holiday in France.

Adam had often thought since that 'Mr Fixer' he might be, but he hadn't been able to prevent that catastrophe. The virus had been too quick for them, and before he'd had the chance to gather his wits his sports-loving, serious young wife had succumbed.

His grief was under control now, and had been for a long time. He knew there were those, including his father, who thought he should be thinking of marrying again, but Adam had found that work was the best antidote against loneliness.

At least that was what he told himself, but there were times when a can of soup at some ungodly hour made him feel that there had to be more to life than that.

The woman with long legs, honey-coloured hair and eyes the colour of bluebells was experiencing excitement tempered with amusement as she was introduced to a predominantly male gathering of the paediatric staff.

The amusement was due to the noticeable stirring of interest when, after announcing her arrival to Personnel, she had presented herself on the unit where she would be working.

Leonie tried not to smile. She had this effect on the opposite sex and invariably treated it with amusement. The times when the boot was on the other foot were rare, although there had been an occasion not so long ago when the man in question hadn't even seemed to be aware of her presence.

It had been at a conference regarding evidence-based medicine that had been held at one of the trust offices. She'd been summoned to attend along with other medical staff and had found on her arrival that it was being chaired by a brisk, dark-haired stranger who had immediately claimed her interest.

Accustomed to being noticed because of her height,

looks and lissom appeal, Leonie had realised as the meeting had progressed that to this man she was just a face, a necessary body amongst others to be made use of, but only with regard to business, and she'd been amazed how his disinterested manner had intrigued her.

A comment to another participant at the conference had led to her being informed that Adam Lockhart was in love with his job, that he'd lost his wife in tragic circumstances and wasn't in the market for a replacement.

The remarks should have wiped out her interest but for some strange reason they hadn't, and she'd wondered if it had been because he was extremely attractive in a controlled sort of way, with hair of thick ebony in a stylish cut, dark, unreadable eyes and an uncompromising mouth that had looked as if smiles graced it rarely.

Or had it been because of the surprise…because she'd been of less note to him than the flowers in a vase in the centre of the table or the utilitarian light fittings of the conference chamber hanging above their heads?

However, as the evening progressed his cool disregard eventually damped down her interest and she sought no further information about the stranger, telling herself that he could have come from the moon as far as she was concerned. Hadn't she had enough hassle from the opposite sex in her turbulent love life?

When her friend, Joanne Archer, mentioned some weeks later that a vacancy for a paediatrician was being advertised at St Mark's Acute Services Hospital, Leonie applied and every other thought was wiped from her mind as she waited to see if she would be successful.

At the interview she was asked to attend there was an assessor from the Royal College, a high-up executive from the trust, another consultant and the head of Personnel, and it seemed that she found favour with them as she was offered the position of paediatrician in a hospital more prestigious than any she'd worked in previously.

She accepted eagerly, departing from her previous position at a children's hospital in Birmingham without too much regret, and now here she was.

The introductions were over and Derek Griffiths, the elderly consultant in charge of Paediatrics, was about to show her around the unit.

'This hospital has a reputation second to none for efficiency,' he explained. 'We have a clinical services manager who never ignores even the smallest detail. He works ceaselessly for the good of St Mark's and expects everyone else employed here to do the same.'

There'd been a strange intonation in Mr Griffiths's voice, almost as if he was issuing a warning, and Leonie thought that this man to whom she would be answerable was the opposite of Adam Lockhart, who'd not even glanced in her direction. Derek Griffiths was taking in every detail of her appearance, and obviously considered her a dumb blonde.

If he thought that a head of honey-coloured hair and long legs were going to affect her efficiency he had another think coming. She knew the job, was good at it, and if she could make a sick child better she was deeply content.

She'd been a sickly child herself once with chronic asthma. It had stayed with her until her teens and, having spent many a stressful night in the paediatric ward of her local hospital, Leonie understood the fears and stresses that can attack the young mind during the hours of darkness in a strange place.

Derek Griffiths was waiting for her to say something and she wasn't going to disappoint him.

Fixing him with her amazing bluebell eyes, she said coolly, 'I don't recollect the perfectionist in question being at my interview, so I shall look forward to meeting him.'

She was aware that she had some nerve, challenging the

man who would be her boss at their first meeting, but he was doing the same, judging her before he'd had the chance to see her in action.

The elderly consultant cleared his throat. 'I'm sure that you'll be making the acquaintance of Adam Lockhart in the very near future, Dr Marsden,' he told her drily, and motioned for her to follow him along the line of beds that were occupied by his young patients.

'Did I hear my name mentioned?' a voice asked from behind, and when the two doctors turned simultaneously Leonie felt her jaw go slack as the memory of a conference on a cold winter night came crowding back.

His face was expressionless, which had to mean that he hadn't a clue who she was. But, then, he wouldn't have, would he? That night some months ago he had been interested only in the evidence, or lack of it, of the success of certain kinds of treatment.

'Adam, let me introduce Dr Leonie Marsden,' Derek Griffiths was saying, and as Leonie held out a hand, which had suddenly gone limp, Adam eyed her with the same polite indifference as before.

'Pleased to meet you, Dr Marsden,' he said in a voice that wasn't in keeping with his cool exterior. It reminded her of Wales, and poetry, and moonlight nights.

She smiled, and when Leonie Marsden really gave her mind to it the sun seemed to hide its head in shame.

'We've met before,' she told him, aware that her voice wasn't as confident as the dazzling smile she was bestowing upon him.

'Is that so? When?'

'At a conference some months ago.'

'Really?'

'Yes. You were chairing it.'

'Was I?'

Her smile was beginning to waver. Did he have to be so disinterested?

'Leonie has come from a hospital in Birmingham to join our paediatric team,' Derek Griffiths put in.

'Then no doubt we shall be seeing each other again,' Adam Lockhart said with easy dismissiveness. As he turned to go he added, 'It was you I came to see, Derek. I'd like a word when you're free.'

The older man gave a laughing groan. 'Not my budget, I hope.'

'Afraid so,' he was told. 'But it's not all bad news. Last night's finance meeting was lengthy, but there was some light at the end of the tunnel.'

'And did you go out to supper afterwards to celebrate?' the consultant asked with a quizzical smile.

'No, I dined at home. Just the two of us—myself and the tin opener.'

'You must eat with us soon. Mary is always saying I must invite you.'

'Tell her that would be nice. As long as I'm not—'

'Working?'

'Mmm. Lately, my evenings are busier than my days.' With a nod to Leonie, who had been listening to the brief exchange of words between the two men, he made his way along the ward with a long, easy stride and departed through the far door.

Coming out of a planning meeting later that morning, Adam collared Joanne Archer, the nursing manager.

'When are you going to get a new car, Joanne?' he asked casually, knowing that the independent divorcee didn't take kindly to interference.

'As soon as I can afford it,' she snapped. 'I suppose you've heard that it broke down again this morning?'

'Yes, it was mentioned as being the reason for your late arrival.'

'I'm sorry, Adam,' she mumbled, raking her fingers through an auburn mop. 'But it's no joke, having to watch every penny. If my friend, Leonie Marsden, hadn't been available to give me a lift, I don't know when I'd have got here.'

'Ah, yes. The new member of staff. So you're acquainted?'

Joanne smiled wickedly. 'You've already met the beautiful Leonie, have you?'

'We have been introduced, yes, but I didn't know that she was a friend of yours.'

'Leonie and I go back a long way,' she said airily. 'We lived on the same street when we were kids. It was me who told her about the vacancy here. She's been working in Birmingham but has wanted to get back to the Manchester area for some time, and where could be better than St Mark's?'

'Where indeed?' he agreed casually, and with a nod went on his way.

As Leonie drove home that night she was going over the day's events with a mixture of pique and pleasure.

Adam Lockhart was the only man who'd caught her attention in a long time and she'd been amazed to meet him again. His name had never come up in conversation with Joanne, and with the dampener of his disinterest that night at the conference she'd asked no further questions about him.

His sudden appearance at St Mark's had been surprising to say the least. Surprising...yes. Uplifting...no. He had been just as aloof as before and yet her pulses had quickened just as they had last time.

Did she want them to, though? She'd been engaged twice

in the past and had been hurt and angry when both relationships had floundered because the men involved hadn't
been able to see further than her physical attractions.
Neither had looked for the woman beneath, the intelligent,
caring doctor who wanted to be loved for her mind as well
as her body.

The experiences had left her very wary, and until the
night when she'd entered the orbit of the manager of St
Mark's Hospital Leonie had foreseen her future stretching
in front of her as a long, lonely road.

And why did she think this man might be different?
From what she'd seen of him so far, he was at the other
extreme to her two fiancés. Had she done the dance of the
seven veils in front of him she doubted if he would have
noticed.

Had she made a mistake, changing jobs? Coming into
contact with a man who seemed happy enough with his
present lifestyle? It had been clear back on the ward that
he hadn't remembered her and in a way she supposed she
should have been thankful. At least *he* hadn't been bowled
over by her outer packaging.

The memory of their stilted meeting brought with it the
more uplifting parts of the day which were just as deeply
imprinted on her consciousness. That first tour of the paediatric unit. Observing the children who would be in her
care. Young sufferers who either by accident or illness had
been brought to St Mark's.

Little Freddie, who only the day before had been dragged
almost lifeless out of a garden pond and was being kept in
for observation in case of unexpected after-effects such as
water having got into the bloodstream.

And eight-year-old Shona McBride who'd run in front
of a car some weeks previously and had suffered multiple
fractures. Leonie had wanted to take her pale little face
between her hands and tell her that it was going to be all

right, but Derek Griffiths had been already moving towards the next bed and she'd had to content herself with a reassuring smile in the little girl's direction.

Today had been all about settling in, meeting the rest of the staff and memorising the layout of the place. Tomorrow she would be in the thick of it and that was how she liked it to be.

If she'd been thrown by the presence of Adam Lockhart, at least she had no regrets about the job. St Mark's was a bigger, more prestigious hospital than anywhere she'd worked previously, as Derek Griffiths had been so quick to point out, and that in itself should be challenge enough.

The move from Birmingham had been rushed and Leonie had taken the first suitable accommodation that had come her way. Her friend, Joanne, had managed to find time to go house-hunting with her, and the two women had agreed that a smart apartment in a refurbished Manchester warehouse only a few minutes' drive from St Mark's would be ideal for both work and play.

As she put her key in the lock Leonie was thankful for the short ride home. A long drive through rush-hour traffic at the end of a working day was no one's idea of happiness.

She'd taken the apartment furnished, and as she looked around her its tasteful decor had a soothing effect after the hustle and bustle of the busy hospital.

After a quick bite she might take in a theatre, she decided. It was too good a chance to miss. Once she was into the thick of things at St Mark's, she might be too tired, or not have the time.

When she'd been in Manchester, house-hunting some weeks earlier, David Threlfall had been appearing in *Peer Gynt* at the resurrected Exchange Theatre.

What was on tonight she didn't know, but if that production was anything to go by, the theatre's standards of excellence were clearly geared to the artistic palate of an enthusiastic patron like herself.

As Leonie was zipping herself into a black dress and easing on her most elegant pair of shoes at the same time, the phone rang.

She tensed. Only personnel at St Mark's, Joanne and one other person knew her number. She picked up the receiver.

'Leonie?'

The smooth, professional tone was familiar and she took a deep breath.

'Yes?'

'James Morgan here. I know it's a bit late in the day to be ringing you, but the results of your tests have just come through and I thought you'd want to know.'

Leonie sank onto the nearest chair. It was the kind of moment she'd been involved in on many occasions, but this time the boot was on the other foot. She was the patient.

'Yes. I do, James,' she told him stiffly, her heartbeat quickening.

Over recent months she'd been having headaches and periods of breathlessness, along with general tiredness, and, after initially putting it down to the rigours of hospital life, had finally decided during her last weeks at the Birmingham hospital that maybe there was some other reason for her not being her usual healthy self.

She'd consulted James Morgan, a haematologist, and now the busy doctor was on the line with the results of the blood tests which he'd asked to be done on her behalf.

'Has anyone in your family ever had to have their spleen removed?' he was asking.

Leonie stared into the receiver.

'Not that I know of. Why?'

'The tests show that it's spherocytosis, a form of inherited haemolytic anaemia. You'll have come across it before, I imagine. It comes from a faulty gene.'

'Yes. I have,' she said slowly. 'It's when there are a lot of small, round blood cells around—spherocytes. But I can't imagine where I might have inherited it from.'

'Maybe you're the first in your family to have it. In all these types of illnesses there has to be someone to start it off.'

His voice had softened, and she had a vision of kind brown eyes in a long face that belied the smooth professionalism of his previous tone.

'And so what happens next?' she asked.

'If your general health doesn't improve I would suggest removal of the spleen, but I think you could carry on as you are for the time being. Especially as you've just started a new job.

'But bear in mind that the symptoms of the condition will worsen if you get any sort of infection and you'll need immediate antibiotics. In the meantime, I suggest that you have the pneumonia vaccine as a possible safeguard.'

'So you think I'm all right to carry on as I am for the time being?'

'Yes. But do take care, Leonie.' His voice was even gentler now. 'You do know that any children you might have could inherit the rogue gene or genes?'

The colour was draining from her face. Yes, she did know that, but in the shock of hearing James's diagnosis she hadn't had time to assimilate that bleak fact.

'Did you hear what I said?' he was asking into the silence.

'Yes, I heard. It's something that I shall have to give a lot of thought to at some distant date.'

'So there are no wedding bells likely in the near future?'

'Not with my track record,' she told him flatly, thinking that this latest development would really put the dampener on any future matrimonial prospects. Two broken engagements had been bad enough, but this was in a class of its own.

When James had hung up she sat, gazing sombrely into space, all thoughts of the theatre forgotten.

All right, treated with respect, the illness wasn't exactly life-threatening as long as she didn't succumb to any vile infections, but there was the possible removal of her spleen looming up, and prior to that the fact that there would be times when she wouldn't be feeling her best while treating the children in her care.

But for the present she could cope with that. Just as long as she was able to fulfil her commitment to St Mark's. It would be just too embarrassing to have to confess to bodily frailty the moment she had become acquainted with the man who had his finger on the pulse of that same hospital.

It was a typical May evening, with a bright sun slanting through the office window as Adam cleared his desk for the day. He'd had a late meeting scheduled but, feeling unaccountably restless, he'd asked his deputy, Mike Stacey, to attend in his place.

A cool morning had turned into a mellow afternoon, and as the day had progressed Adam had felt a sudden yearning to get home to the boat.

The Apple hadn't seen much of him lately. It rarely did. It was a fact of life. The life he lived, anyway. But today he craved the tranquillity of the marina and the comforting movement of his home as it rocked gently on the water.

As he drove towards it through the Cheshire countryside, an incident earlier in the day plagued his mind. He'd allowed the new doctor on Paediatrics to think he didn't remember them having met before but, of course, he did.

Leonie Marsden was far too attractive to go anywhere unobserved, even by the likes of himself. That day at the conference there hadn't been a man in the room who hadn't been impressed by her style and stunning good looks.

Had it been a small gathering, they would, no doubt, have been acquainted by the time it was over, but the conference room had been packed.

He'd been in the chair, bogged down with the procedures on hand, and it had been easy to use that as the excuse not to get to know the most attractive woman in the room.

By the time he'd managed to disentangle himself from the verbal grip of various members of the trust at the end of the conference, she'd gone, and in keeping with the lifestyle he'd adopted since losing Annabel he'd made no effort to find out who she was.

But today they'd met again and she was just as memorable. Paler, thinner, maybe, but still incredibly attractive.

'Your concerns should be with her performance on the wards and in the clinics,' he told himself with a wry smile. 'Handsome is as handsome does…and in any case a woman like that has got to be in a relationship. How do you know that husband and kids weren't waiting for her tonight, eager to know how Mum had coped with her first day at St Mark's?'

By the time Leonie arrived at the hospital the next morning she had adjusted to the disturbing news from James Morgan. She'd decided that there were far worse things she could have had wrong with her than spherocytosis. It might have been some deadly form of leukaemia or suchlike.

A sensible lifestyle and taking care to avoid infection should keep her off the operating table for some time to come. The last thing she wanted was for Adam Lockhart to see her as some sort of ailing passenger on his staff. Derek Griffiths had said that Adam was efficiency personified and expected those employed at St Mark's to be the same.

However, adjusting to the diagnosis she'd been given wasn't so easy when it came to accepting the fact that it was an inherited illness.

Even though she was certain that she must be the first in her family to have the rogue gene, it wasn't the past that concerned her.

The future was what mattered. The thought that she could blight the lives of any children she might give birth to was a devastating thought. She'd seen the effects of genetic mistakes countless times amongst little ones she'd treated, and now nature was playing a similar trick on herself.

In a smart navy blazer and grey trousers, and with the long golden swathe of her hair in a thick plait that swung gently to and fro as she moved, the casual observer could have been forgiven for thinking that here was a woman at the height of her allure.

That she was a hard-working paediatrician with a worrying ailment that could soon swerve out of control would have been the last thought to come to mind.

Adam Lockhart's office was on the ground floor. She had to pass it to get to Paediatrics and, unable to help herself, Leonie took a long, hard look through the glass-panelled door.

It was empty—the desk uncluttered, the carpet fluffless and the window open to let in the fresh morning air. So where was he, the man who kept the huge hospital working on all cylinders?

Approaching with the apparent speed of light, from the looks of it. He was moving swiftly towards her along the corridor with a briefcase in hand and a look on his face that didn't match the bright morning.

His step slowed to a more normal walk when he saw her hovering outside his door and she felt her face go warm.

'Leonie?' he questioned unsmilingly. 'Are you waiting to see me? Problems already?'

She smiled. If he'd got out of the wrong side of the bed she wasn't going to be guilty of casting doom and gloom around, and today, with the new knowledge of her illness, she had an excuse if anybody had.

'The answer is no to both questions,' she said lightly. 'I'm not waiting to see you and there are no problems...at least none that you could help me with.'

His face was lightening. 'That makes a change. Most people think I have a magic wand that will solve everything. Create extra beds when there's a shortage. Put money into the hospital coffers when they're empty. Reduce waiting lists. I could go on for ever.'

'And who solves your problems, Adam?' she asked softly, aware that she was being a trifle familiar with the big chief of hospital management.

There was surprise in the dark eyes looking into hers, and Leonie thought that either she was indeed being over-familiar with the man who was the guardian of St Mark's, or Adam Lockhart wasn't used to anyone contemplating that he might be human enough to have frailties of his own.

'I put them up on the shelf and hope they'll go away,' he said drily, with his hand on the doorhandle of his office. Leonie saw that she'd been dismissed. The king was anxious to set himself upon his throne. Affairs of state were being neglected while he gossiped with a mere mortal.

'I see,' she said, and with a casual wave of the hand she began to move away. 'Bye for now.'

The early finish of the night before hadn't done anything to banish Adam's restlessness. He'd sat out on deck until very late and arisen with a rare reluctance to get mobile.

As he'd gone through the motions of shaving and dressing he'd questioned whether it was the time of year that was affecting him—early summer with its promise of new life, new beginnings.

Or if his reluctance to sally forth to St Mark's was because of Leonie Marsden's appearance on the scene.

His personal life was simple and uncluttered, and until yesterday he'd thought that was how he wanted it to stay.

CHAPTER TWO

THERE was no sign of Derek Griffiths when Leonie arrived at the two children's wards, which were situated off the hospital's main corridor.

No doubt the head of Paediatrics felt that he'd done his bit the day before, showing her around and introducing her to the staff.

Now she would be expected to slot herself into the running of the unit and get cracking, and as there wasn't an empty bed to be seen there was going to be plenty to occupy her.

Two young nurses who hadn't been present the previous day were doing the rounds with the drugs trolley to a familiar accompaniment of childish chatter and plaintive wailing, and as Leonie approached the ward office she could see the dark head of the sister in charge bent over the night staff's reports.

There was a junior doctor hovering beside her and as Leonie appeared in the doorway they both looked up. She recognised him from the previous day and there was the same warmth in his eyes as there had been then, but his companion's expression was more guarded.

Leonie wasn't to know that it was Sister Beth Carradine's first morning back after a week's leave. She'd been looking forward to returning to her young charges and the company of Simon Harris, who'd been showing signs of fancying her as much as she fancied him.

But, after asking briefly if she'd enjoyed the break, Simon's one topic of conversation since entering the office had been the arrival the previous day of a stunning new doctor on the unit. And now here she was, blonde and very beautiful.

The look in Sister Carradine's eyes was one that Leonie was used to seeing. Where her appearance invariably evoked admiration and interest from the opposite sex, those of her own gender were apt to eye her with less enthusiasm.

They often saw her as the enemy, an alien force to be reckoned with, making her want to explain that it wasn't so. She hadn't chosen the combination of genes that made her look as she did…just as she wasn't responsible for the one that was already putting a blight on her life.

With her hand outstretched she moved towards the solemn girl behind the desk. 'Leonie Marsden reporting for duty, Sister.' She nodded at the man at her side. 'We've already met, haven't we? Dr Harris, isn't it?'

'Yes, I'm Simon Harris,' he said enthusiastically. 'I've been told that I'm to accompany you on ward rounds, Dr Marsden.'

'Fine,' she said easily, aware of the sister's wary hazel gaze. 'And you, too, Sister, I hope. I'm going to need you to put me in the picture. I saw most of the children briefly yesterday, but didn't get time to familiarise myself with their problems.' She stepped back, indicating that Beth should lead the way. 'So, shall we commence?'

As they moved from bed to bed Leonie listened carefully to what they had to say, asking questions when she thought necessary and treating the young patients with friendly gentleness.

With Simon, who was positively goggling, she was polite but aloof, and when they met back in the office afterwards to discuss any possible problems or treatment needed, Leonie sensed that the sister was feeling less threatened.

Perching herself on the corner of the desk, she informed them, 'From what I see, we have the usual run of children's ailments that require hospitalisation, along with a smattering of really serious cases, which is what one usually finds on a paediatric ward.

'Tell me about Miles Anderton, Sister. How long has he been in St Mark's?'

'Since the day he was born, three years ago,' Beth told her. 'As you saw from his notes, Dr Marsden, Miles has many problems—all of them grave.'

'They are indeed,' Leonie agreed. 'Has anyone had any thoughts about him being sent home for a trial period?'

'It's under discussion. Mr Griffiths has mentioned it, but it will mean full-time attention around the clock for him, with nurses and carers to assist his parents.'

Leonie nodded thoughtfully. The child they were discussing had been in Intensive Care for the first two and a half years of his life and was now in the transitional care unit.

Born with a rare neuromuscular condition, Miles was still unable to walk or swallow and required help with breathing. He had always been fed through a tube and his only form of mobility was in a small electric wheelchair.

The hospital was the only home he had ever known and as soon as she'd seen him Leonie had wondered what the future held for the toddler.

The problems facing St Mark's and his parents if he were to be discharged would be great, but from what she'd just been told he might go home one day.

Alexandra Cottrell was another seriously ill child in paediatric care, and Leonie had spent a long time beside her bed. The eleven-month-old baby girl's heart had become enlarged from an unknown virus and time was running out for her. A heart transplant was needed and so far no donor had been found.

Her distraught parents had been beside her, and as Leonie had examined the pallid child the signs of heart failure had all been there.

'They keep telling us that there have been some amazingly successful results in transplant operations on very young children,' Alexandra's father had said raggedly, 'but it doesn't help if no heart is going to become available, does it?'

Leonie had nodded her agreement. It didn't help and, added to that, in those sort of cases there was always the knowledge that when an organ did appear it meant great sorrow for someone else.

At that moment the phone rang, and when the ward sister had answered it she said, 'It's Mr Lockhart's secretary for you, Dr Marsden.'

'Jean Telfer here,' a voice said in her ear when Leonie took the receiver from Beth. 'Mr Lockhart would like to see you in his office when you are free, Dr Marsden.'

'Er...right. I'll come now,' she said. 'I've just finished ward rounds and have a few moments to spare.'

Leaving Beth Carradine and her staff to carry on with the running of the children's wards, Leonie made her way to Adam Lockhart's office with a half-smile on her lips.

It was like being at school and receiving a summons to the headmaster's office, but in this instance Adam Lockhart didn't have a receding hairline and glasses.

He was dark and interesting in a restrained sort of way. Goods not for the touching of, if what she'd seen of him so far was correct. And that being so, why was she so interested?

It was as if the man lived behind a barrier of reserve. Maybe tragedy and loss had that effect on some people. But she was making snap judgements, wasn't she?

So far she'd been in Adam's company just three times, hardly long enough to be deciding what did or didn't make him tick.

Yet one thing was abundantly clear. He wasn't panting to get to know her in any sense other than her usefulness to St Mark's, and, no doubt, the summons to his royal presence was related to that fact.

She could hear laughter coming from inside his office as she approached, and her step faltered. Adam had someone with him and from the sound of the spontaneous mirth she'd caught him in a light-hearted moment.

The sound of a footstep behind had her turning, and she found an elderly woman in a neat grey suit observing her over gold-rimmed spectacles.

'Dr Marsden, isn't it?' Jean Telfer questioned. 'Do go in. He's expecting you.' As Leonie hesitated, she added, 'It's nothing private. Only the nursing manager, regaling Mr Lockhart with the latest exploits of her young rascals.'

As Leonie did her bidding she saw Joanne standing by his desk while Adam was hunched behind it, his eyes brimming with laughter and his shoulders shaking.

When he saw her he straightened up, sobering instantly, and Leonie had the feeling that she'd interrupted a special moment. If she had, Joanne wasn't giving the game away.

'Hi, there,' her friend said breezily. 'How's it going, Leonie?'

'Fine,' she said with equal nonchalance, and as Joanne moved towards the door Leonie seated herself on the chair to which Adam was pointing.

'I imagine you're wondering why I've sent for you,' he said as soon as the door had closed behind the other woman.

'Yes. I am rather.'

'I just wanted a quick chat, that's all. On the two other occasions we've met since your arrival here it wasn't the right moment, but as we've both got a little time to spare maybe now it is.'

Leonie crossed the long legs that always seemed to create such interest in male onlookers and waited.

'I hope that you'll be happy here at St Mark's, Dr

Marsden,' he said smoothly. 'We have an excellent team, from our top consultants and administrators to the porters, auxiliary staff, cleaners and so on.

'If any one of them ever has a problem I demand to hear about it. Unrest and frustration only fester, and the sooner the healing process is under way the better the service we give.'

Her eyes widened as, with his gaze on some point on the Manchester skyline visible through the window, he said quietly, 'I envy you the privilege of caring for the young sick of St Mark's. I can't think of anything more rewarding than helping some of them back to health and happiness. Do you have children of your own?'

Leonie felt her jaw go slack. Was he crazy? Hadn't he seen her records? Or was he indicating that the unmarried state didn't necessarily describe a situation of childless-ness...for someone like her.

'No, I don't. You may have seen from my records that I'm single,' she told him with chilly politeness. 'And as to my job, I'm sure that my part in health care can be no greater than the huge contribution that you make yourself.'

The moment was becoming unreal. Or was the way it was turning out only to be expected? That he was more inclined to congratulate her on her function in health care than having hair like buttermilk and eyes as blue as a sum-mer sky, which was how one ardent admirer had once de-scribed them.

He changed the subject.

'When we met earlier and I asked if you had problems, you hinted that you might have, but that they weren't of the kind that hospital management could help with. Am I right?'

Where was this leading? she wondered. She was hardly going to tell this brisk perfectionist that only time would show how well her body was going to cope with the gene fault that had recently come to light.

She didn't want him to be forever watching her, judging her performance in his beloved hospital. It would be like starting her career at St Mark's with a millstone around her neck.

'Yes. You're right,' she told him with reluctant truth. 'I do have a problem…and it isn't anything you can help me with. If you're concerned that it might affect my efficiency you needn't be. I would resign immediately if those circumstances should arise.'

Leonie was beginning to feel irritated now. She'd barely set foot in the place before she was being given the third degree. Was this regular practice, or was it only reserved for leggy blondes who were too eye-catching for their own good?

The only people who knew about the spherocytosis were James Morgan, the consultant at Birmingham, and herself. She hadn't told Joanne, mainly because she didn't want to worry her friend and because the resilient divorcee had enough problems of her own.

She was glad now that she hadn't, as it meant Adam Lockhart wasn't going to discover that a member of his staff was suffering from a genetic illness from that source.

'Fair enough,' he said levelly, 'but remember that part of my function here is to see that staff are worry-free as much as possible, enabling them to give of their best in whatever role they have to play.'

'I'll bear that in mind,' she said coolly, with the feeling that because the clinical services manager of St Mark's Hospital had no other outlets for his energy, he expected those working for him to be the same, putting the hospital first…before everything else.

He was getting to his feet. 'Joanne tells me that you're friends from way back and that it was she who put you onto the vacancy here. What made you decide to leave your previous position?'

Leonie could imagine his expression were she to say, You would have been the reason if I'd known you were here. You're the first man I've met who hasn't drooled over me. I would have seen you as a challenge.

Instead, she told him truthfully, 'St Mark's has a brilliant reputation. I've always wanted to work here. When I got the chance, I took it.'

When Leonie Marsden had gone Adam seated himself once more and closed his eyes. A fine mess he'd made of that.

What on earth had possessed him to ask her if she'd got children when it stated clearly on her records that she wasn't married?

Yesterday he'd not had the chance to glance over them but this morning he'd remedied the omission and had seen that she was unmarried. Not divorced or widowed but unmarried, which was an amazing state of affairs, considering her attractions. She must have thought his question either crazy or quite insulting.

And why had he gone burbling on about how he envied the staff who worked at the coal face. She must have thought him a complete whinger. He didn't envy them at all. It was everyone to his or her function and in running the hospital to its present standard of efficiency he was more than fulfilling his.

Yet he'd had to talk to her about something. She was one of the most beautiful women he'd ever seen and yet seemed unaware of it, or if she was she gave no sign. Just as he wasn't prepared to let her see how much she was affecting him.

He was putting it down to having not sought the company of the opposite sex in a personal sense for so long and then suddenly being faced with a delicacy so tempting that if he didn't watch it he would be hungering for large slices.

There'd been shadows beneath the incredible blue eyes, and in spite of her beauty she'd been very pale. He would be watching her from now on and, surprisingly, it would be mostly for her own sake and not with St Mark's in mind.

Leonie returned to the paediatric unit in a bemused state after the strange interview with Adam Lockhart. Did he always see new staff in his office, she wondered, or had that performance been especially for her?

If so, why? Surely the man wasn't so wrapped up in the excellence of the hospital that he concerned himself over his staff's personal problems? Or was he just inquisitive?

She doubted it. There was an aloofness about him that indicated that he kept his affairs close to his chest and had no objection to other folks doing the same, just as long as it didn't affect the love of his life—St Mark's.

Though there'd been nothing aloof about the way he'd been chatting with Joanne. It had been easy to see they were on very good terms but, then, her friend had known Adam Lockhart a lot longer and the resilient, flame-haired nursing manager had her own sort of appeal.

Back on the ward there'd been a discharge and a new admission. A child recovering from a severe attack of croup had been sent home and a young boy with a scalded foot had been placed in the empty bed for observation, after being treated in Accident and Emergency.

Derek Griffiths had appeared from wherever he'd been and when he saw her the senior consultant said, 'I shall be in Theatre for most of the afternoon, Dr Marsden, with Paul Conway, who is also a paediatric surgeon, and young Dr Harris to assist.'

He indicated an eleven-year-old girl, lying lethargically beneath a notice, NIL BY MOUTH. 'That young lady is due to have surgery for the removal of her appendix at two o'clock. But first I'm going to do a laparoscopy as she's suddenly free of the severe pain that was present when they brought her in. As we both know, that's not a good sign when dealing with appendicitis.'

Hunger and the morning's activities were bringing on fatigue and, after buying a sandwich and a canned drink in the snack bar, Leonie went outside into the midday sun to have her lunch.

There was a small, flower-filled garden not far from the paediatric unit and she settled herself on a wooden bench there and began to eat. Across the way were the dark waters of the Irwell and on the far side a riverside restaurant was doing a busy trade with office workers and shoppers.

As she watched the comings and goings of its lunchtime trade, her attention was caught by a familiar figure.

Adam Lockhart was seated at a table on a paved area beside the river with a meal and a glass of beer in front of him. As if he sensed that she was watching him, he looked up.

She could see surprise in his manner. Then he got to his feet and came to stand at the water's edge.

'Would you care to join me?' he called across, indicating the curved wooden bridge that joined the restaurant fore-court with the hospital grounds.

Leonie hesitated. She would like nothing better, even though their meeting earlier in the day had left her some-what confused, but she'd got her own food. It wasn't the done thing to dine on someone else's premises without making a purchase of some sort.

He apparently read her mind. 'I'll buy you a drink.'

She got to her feet. In twenty minutes she was due back. It was long enough to have a non-alcoholic beverage and a quick chat with the enigmatic hospital manager.

'And so how has your first morning in at the deep end

gone?' he asked when they'd sorted out what she was going to have to drink.

Leonie stifled a groan. So they were still going to be talking shop.

'Fine,' she said breezily. 'I'm still feeling my way of course, but, yes, it's going very well.'

He nodded and then, as if to prove wrong her assumptions about it being business as usual, asked, 'Where do you live, Leonie? Not too far away, I hope.'

She smiled. 'Anything but. I have an apartment just off Whitworth Street in the city centre.'

'What's it like?'

She gave him a quick sideways glance. Was this an exercise in putting a new member of staff at ease—or was he really interested?

'Excellent. The development, which was once a warehouse, has its own gymnasium, indoor pool and various other amenities—and I'm not far from the Exchange Theatre.'

'Lucky you. I'm a keen theatre-goer myself. Perhaps you could keep me informed of what's on? Although my problem is that I have so many evening meetings. Such a lot of decisions on health care have to be made after normal working hours.'

'So you don't have much time to yourself?'

'That's the name of the game,' he admitted wryly.

It was her turn to be curious. 'And where do you live, Adam?'

His face softened at the question and for a second he looked dreamy and vulnerable. 'Heaven! I live in heaven, Leonie. On a houseboat called *The Adam's Apple*. It's moored on a quiet marina in the Cheshire countryside just a few miles from here.'

'Really? That sounds divine!'

His eyes widened. 'You think so? Lots of folk don't. I'm looked upon as some sort of recluse.'

'And are you?'

His dark eyes locked on hers at the question. 'I suppose I am, up to a point,' he admitted slowly, 'in that I live a rather solitary life. But after a day in the thick of it at St Mark's the boat is a haven of peace.'

At least it had been until a couple of days ago, he thought as his glance fastened on the pale curve of her throat and a mouth that was made for kisses.

'So you prefer to live alone?' she questioned casually.

'I have done so far. Yes. Do I take it that the same applies to you?'

His tone was as casual as her own and Leonie felt a perverse urge to liven up the discussion.

'I don't exactly live alone from choice. I have no close family and as all the men I meet seem to see me as fair game I'm wary of relationships.'

'You're quite safe with me,' he said flatly, and she wished she could take the words back. Whatever had possessed her to say such a thing? It might be true, but Adam Lockhart was the last person she should be telling that. To him she was merely a piece of equipment for the use of.

It would seem that the only liaison this man wanted was with the big ticking heart that beat inside the building just across from where they were sitting.

Leonie got to her feet. 'I have to go. I'll be the only doctor on the ward this afternoon.'

'Me, too,' he agreed. 'Just as soon as I've paid the bill.'

She paused with one foot on the curve of the bridge and with a crazy desire to test just how much he did want to be left alone she said, 'I'd love to see your boat some time.'

The waiter was approaching his table and Adam had his head turned towards him as she spoke, but at her words he swung slowly round to face her.

'Would you really? It hasn't got a gymnasium, you know.'

Leonie laughed. 'Maybe not. But it's certainly got its own pool.' With a casual wave of the hand she left him to pay for his meal.

The appendectomy wasn't as straightforward as Derek Griffiths would have liked. The laparoscopy had shown that the appendix had burst, and once the incision had been made in the lower abdomen the infected area of the cavity had to be washed out with saline and a drainage tube inserted to clear away any pus.

'Do you know why I told the nurses that the child wasn't to be given a pre-op enema?' Derek asked Simon Harris when the young patient was in Recovery.

When Simon didn't answer immediately the elderly consultant turned to Leonie who had just joined them. 'Tell him, Dr Marsden.'

'An enema could cause peristalsis, the rhythmic movement that propels food and waste products through the digestive system, and that's something a surgeon can do without when performing an appendectomy,' she explained with a sympathetic smile for the young doctor.

Derek nodded his agreement and went on to say, 'If this had been a straightforward appendectomy I would have layered the skin back into position once we'd removed the appendix. But as there's a drainage tube in place, that isn't possible. Antibiotic irrigation will be applied, and when the drain is removed in approximately forty-eight hours the wound should seal itself.'

When he had departed Simon said dolefully, 'I made myself look a complete fool, didn't I?'

Leonie shook her head. 'Don't worry about it. We're all inclined to clam up in the company of the great ones.'

The young doctor might be best kept at arm's length in

another situation, but in this instance she couldn't help but treat him kindly.

She'd gone through it herself—some older man who knew it all, trying her out to see what she knew. And yet that was what it was all about—looking and learning from experience and reading the printed pages, hundreds of them.

In a meeting in another part of the building Adam was doing what he did best, often with his back to the wall—fighting for resources, negotiating for the funds needed to keep the hospital running at top efficiency.

For once, however, his mind wasn't as firmly on the matter in hand as it usually was. Leonie had said she'd like to see the boat and, surprisingly, he hadn't resorted to the cool detachment he usually relied on when acquaintances attempted to muscle into his private life.

In fact, he'd felt a surge of pleasure at the thought of showing her around his beloved *Apple*, and was still wondering why he hadn't immediately taken her up on her suggestion.

When the meeting was over he found himself moving in the direction of the paediatric unit and knew why. He wanted to see her again to extend the invitation he'd been slow to offer earlier in the day. But a tearful young boy and his mother were moving in the same direction. Catching them up, he asked quietly of the harassed woman, 'Can I help? You seem to have a problem.'

She eyed him uncertainly. 'I don't know. Who are you? You're not a doctor, are you?'

Adam smiled. 'No, I'm not, but I am employed here. Shall we say I'm the organiser in chief?'

He face cleared. 'Oh, I see,' she said, and then she sighed. 'Our Josh is due to be admitted to the children's ward and he's not happy. He's got some sort of heart problem but nobody is telling us what it is.'

'Maybe that's because they don't know,' Adam said gently. 'I presume you've brought him in for tests?'

'Er, yes, I have.'

'Right. That's why no one is telling you anything, but they will once they know if there's anything wrong.'

The child's wailing had dwindled to a sniffle and Adam took him by the hand. 'Come along, Josh,' he coaxed. 'There's no need to cry. We're going to make you better if there's something wrong, and if there isn't your mum can take you home. In the meantime, we've got lots of games for you to play with and there are other children like you who have come here to be made better.'

Leonie's eyes widened when she saw Adam appear, holding the hand of the tear-stained child, with his mother trailing behind like a nervous bridesmaid. Her amazement increased when he went up to Beth Carradine and asked her to keep him informed of the little one's progress.

As he turned to go the mother beamed her gratitude and Leonie thought that perhaps he wasn't always 'Mr Touch Me Not'. Adam had taken time in the middle of his busy day to reassure a frightened child and his mother.

With that thought came another. He wasn't ever likely to be involved in comforting any child of hers that might be admitted to St Mark's because she wasn't having any.

Her past experiences with the opposite sex were partly responsible for the decision, and had been reinforced since the genetic fault had come to light.

Adam Lockhart might have been the most memorable man she'd ever met but she wasn't going to fall into any traps of her own making.

At the end of the day, as Adam pointed homewards the silver Jaguar, which came second only to the boat in his list of treasured possessions, an open-topped yellow sports car whizzed past on the road outside the hospital. As he watched a mane of golden hair lift in the wind he realised that the invitation still hadn't been voiced, and the quiet evening he'd been looking forward to had suddenly lost its appeal.

After she'd let herself into the apartment Leonie went into her bedroom and lay on the bed. The tiredness she'd been fighting since late afternoon was taking over. Added to that, she felt breathless and slightly nauseous.

It was nothing to be surprised at under the circumstances. They were the symptoms of spherocytosis. As long as she didn't succumb to any infections there was no need to panic. Maybe one day, when she'd settled into her slot at St Mark's and had proved her worth, she could sort out the business of having her spleen removed, but not yet.

The last thing she wanted at the moment was for Adam Lockhart to see her as less than efficient, and as long as she lived sensibly and didn't overdo it there shouldn't be a problem.

It was warm in the room and as her eyelids began to droop she thought wryly that the picture she presented at that moment was a far cry from that of the glamorous sex symbol so many people saw her as.

With drowsiness settling upon her like a comforting blanket, there came the question—how did Adam see her? The man with his finger on the pulse of St Mark's. It was as well he wasn't feeling *her* pulse at that particular moment as its beat was as slow and sluggish as the state of her consciousness.

It had been fast enough back there beside the Irwell in the lunch-hour, though, hadn't it? After she'd asked him to show her his boat. But it had slowed down pretty smartish when there'd been no invitation forthcoming, and for the rest of the afternoon she'd had a sinking feeling that she'd blown it, been too pushy.

But she couldn't be fretting about it at this moment. The tiredness was overwhelming. Tomorrow she would find herself a GP, explain the circumstances of her illness and request the pneumonia vaccine.

She would be all right in the morning—she always was. But was she being fair to herself or her employer, keeping the details of her illness to herself?

CHAPTER THREE

LEONIE did feel better the next morning, reassuringly so, and the doubts and fears of the night before receded.

She accepted that there would be moments when she felt tired and ill, but as long as they weren't too frequent and didn't escalate into something more serious she would be able to cope.

The first person she saw on arriving at St Mark's was Joanne, and as the two women passed the time of day Leonie wondered just how close the nursing manager was to Adam Lockhart.

'I thought you seemed to be on very good terms with Mr Efficiency when I was summoned to his presence yesterday,' she said casually as they walked along the main corridor together.

'Who? Adam?' Joanne questioned, and then, before Leonie could confirm that it was indeed he to whom she'd been referring, she added, 'Yes. I suppose I am, though we do sometimes cross swords. He's always on at me to get a new car. Whether it's because the old banger I'm driving plays havoc with my punctuality on the job, or because he's concerned about my safety on the road, I'm not sure.'

'Maybe it's a bit of both,' Leonie suggested. 'He's not the type to be happy with loose ends in any shape or form, is he?'

'Tell me about it!' Joanne said with a laughing grimace. 'He's even offered to lend me the cash to get a new car.'

'Really! And what did you say?'

'That I'd think it over. Before the divorce I always had a decent car, but money is a lot tighter these days. I'd give my back teeth for a smart little number like yours,' she said with sudden wistfulness. 'It goes so perfectly with your image.'

'What image? Blondie with a stethoscope?'

'It really gets you down, the way your looks affect people, doesn't it?' Joanne said quizzically.

'Yes, it does,' Leonie agreed. 'Don't forget that I've already had two relationships that never really got off the ground because the men concerned didn't see me for what I was…and at this moment in time I'm not looking for any more.'

That wasn't strictly true, of course, but she was hardly going to confess to Joanne that she was attracted to the clinical services manager of St Mark's, especially as Joanne and Adam seemed to be on such good terms.

Yet when they came across him seconds later, standing beside the entrance to the pharmacy, in deep discussion with a middle-aged security guard, it was on her that his dark gaze immediately fastened. In that moment it was as if Joanne and the guard had ceased to exist.

Was he remembering her rash comment that she'd like to see his boat? she wondered as the nursing manager gave him a casual wave and went into her office. Or had the intensity of his dark regard merely been because she was a new member of staff?

Whatever he was thinking, it was apparent that her sudden appearance had opened up some train of thought, but whether it was private or public she wasn't about to discover at that particular moment as, after wishing her a cool good morning, he turned his attention back to the guard and said, 'So the cupboard has definitely been forced?'

'Yes. Afraid so, Mr Lockhart,' the guard replied. 'I'm about to check for any footprints outside the window as that's been forced as well. There was rain during the night so it might show something up on the flower-beds outside.'

'Yes, do that,' Adam agreed, 'and let me know if anything else comes up. I've spoken to the pharmacy staff and they're doing a check on what's been taken.'

'Trouble?' Leonie questioned.

His smile had a grim sort of wryness about it. 'You could say that. There was a break-in last night in the pharmacy— even with all the security precautions I insist on.'

'Didn't the night staff see or hear anything?'

'It would appear not.'

'So your day hasn't started too well,' she said sympathetically.

As Adam observed the slender figure of the young doctor, today dressed in a navy suit with a crisp white blouse, he had a sudden insane urge to tell her that it was improving by the minute, but did he want to join the ranks of those who slobbered over Leonie Marsden? No way!

'I've known worse,' he said drily, with a quick glance at a clock above their heads, 'and if I don't show my face in the next few seconds my secretary will be sending out a search party, as will the paediatric unit.'

'Yes, of course,' she agreed politely. 'I'll be on my way.' She eyed the closed door of Joanne's office. 'I wouldn't want Joanne to have done a day's work before I've even started.' The tart comment had him eyeing her with raised brows as she went on her way.

Had he been hinting that she was dawdling? she wondered as the children's wards came into view. Because if he had he was wrong. She wasn't due on the ward for another fifteen minutes.

So much for her being concerned about his affairs! He could take his boat and...what? Sink it!

There were no further sightings of Adam Lockhart for the rest of the day and, with her mind and hands fully occupied with her small patients, Leonie's annoyance had subsided by the time she was ready to leave at six o'clock.

She did see his secretary, though. Jean Telfer was manoeuvring an old Rover out of the hospital car park as Leonie went to get her buttercup-coloured BMW. The older woman wound down the window.

'How's it going?' she asked. 'Are you settling in?'

'Er...yes, thanks.'

'I'm taking a couple of days off,' the secretary informed her. 'Mr Lockhart left for London on the four o'clock train. He's got a series of meetings in the capital and won't be back until the end of the week, so I'm taking advantage of his absence to arrange one of my own.'

'So his boat will be left unattended?'

'He's told you about *The Adam's Apple*?' Jean asked in surprise, and Leonie wondered whatever had possessed her to say such a thing.

'He did mention it, yes.'

'The craft will be safe enough. The other people who have houseboats on the Three Masts Marina will be around, and he always leaves it securely locked up,' Jean Telfer informed her, with her surprise still showing.

'Yes, of course,' Leonie agreed casually, and as Adam's secretary went on her way an idea was born. She was curious to see where he lived. What better time to view the outside of his floating palace than when he was away? If an invitation to visit wasn't going to be forthcoming she would do a survey of her own.

It would be an opportunity to visualise the man in his own particular 'heaven', as he'd described it, and as she was becoming more intrigued with him it was important that she did so.

He would never know she'd been, which was perhaps as well since he'd admitted that he did have reclusive tendencies, but maybe she could change that...given the chance.

* * *

The marina was on a canal basin in a pretty Cheshire village that made the upmarket apartments in Manchester's city centre look like Alcatraz.

A map of the local countryside had guided Leonie to its location and, after parking the car nearby, she had gone to stand by the water's edge.

It was a typical May evening, with the sun still sweeping across the sky and a balmy breeze rippling the waters that led to distant locks.

There were people pottering on the boats and along the canalside, but their presence didn't interfere with the lazy tranquillity of the scene. He'd described the place as 'heaven' and rightly so. She envied him.

Four houseboats were moored there and *The Adam's Apple* was by far the most striking craft. She smiled. It would have to be, wouldn't it? Adam Lockhart wasn't the type to be happy living in an old tub. Even the decks were gleaming.

Through a large window at the stern she could see a lounge area furnished in warm cream and terracotta, and through a side opening there was a glimpse of a neat galley.

Her smile came back as she thought that he was on his way to London at that moment, which was just as well. She could imagine his expression if he were to catch her here...snooping.

In the next second Leonie discovered that imagination wasn't called for. He was there beside her, looking anything but pleased.

'Adam!' she squeaked. 'I thought you were in London.'

'Obviously. What are you doing here?'

She stiffened. Anyone would have thought he'd caught her breaking and entering!

'I was under the impression that English waterways are for public use. I'm not trespassing, I hope.'

'No, of course not,' he said curtly. 'But why come here

when I'm absent? I don't bite, you know. I would have invited you, given the chance.'

'It was curiosity that brought me here—that's all,' she said lamely, knowing it to be not strictly true, but she was hardly going to tell him that every single thing about him was of interest to her.

'I wouldn't have known where to come if your secretary hadn't mentioned this place when we spoke as I was leaving St Mark's earlier...and why *aren't* you in London?'

'My train was cancelled. So, instead of catching a later one, I decided to spend the night at home and travel on the first that's running in the morning.'

That had been four hours ago. Had that occurred to her? he wondered. Did the curiosity she'd referred to have her questioning where he'd been since?

The answer was that he'd had a meal in the city centre, instead of rushing home as he would normally have done, and then had gone for a stroll along Whitworth Street to see for himself the apartment block where Leonie lived...only to find, on returning home, that their minds had been working along the same lines.

He'd seen the yellow sports car first, parked in the lane, and had goggled at it in some astonishment. And now here she was, beside the water, in a blue dress that matched her incredible eyes...and he wasn't pleased.

If she was going to view his boat he'd wanted to be there, showing her around, taking note of her reactions, generally playing the host. But for some reason Leonie Marsden had come out here behind his back.

It was quite clear that Adam Lockhart wasn't overjoyed to find her here, Leonie was telling herself. She had invaded his privacy and he didn't like it.

Having already decided that it wouldn't be wise to let him see just how much anything connected with him gripped her, she turned away, telling him with unconscious wistfulness, 'I'm sorry I've intruded into your tranquil backwater. It's plain to see why you love it here. The place is delightful. As you have to be up at crack of dawn, I'll be on my way.'

She was going and Adam knew now that he didn't want that.

'As you're already here, why not come inside?' he said in a milder, more inviting tone. 'I can't offer to feed you, as a well-stocked larder doesn't go with my lifestyle…and in any case I've already eaten.'

'So have I,' she informed him.

'Then come along. You can tell me what you think of *The Apple* when I've shown you round.'

She was weakening. Adam was entitled to be peeved, after finding her nosing around, and if she didn't accept this invitation there mightn't be another.

He took her hand and began to lead her towards the gangplank. She didn't resist. The contact was electric, his clasp like coming home. Was he experiencing the same sensations? She wished she knew.

The light was fading and she was still there, sitting on deck beside him with a long drink in her hand, watching the setting sun sink below the horizon and wishing that she could stay there for ever.

'So you like *The Apple*?' Adam questioned with his eyes on her face.

'How could you doubt it?' she said softly.

She'd been captivated by the whole place. Her glimpse of the sitting room through the window hadn't done it justice. It was a tasteful, relaxing sort of room with comfortable furniture and bright rugs scattered over the polished wooden floor.

The bedroom below deck, set out in traditional cabin style, with a large double bed in the middle and the portholes made into small feature windows, was just as eye-catching.

It was plain to see that a lot of time and effort had gone into the designing of *The Apple*, and Leonie wondered if it had been a kind of therapy, something to take Adam's mind off sorrow and loss.

He was very still. In the fading light she couldn't see his face, but his shirt gleamed whitely and she thought guiltily that she hadn't given him the opportunity to change out of the clothes he'd worn for work.

An owl hooted in nearby woods, and as the haunting magic of the night wrapped itself around her she knew it would be easy to succumb to it were the man beside her equally affected, but that was crazy thinking.

Adam was putting up with her company because she'd more or less foisted herself on him. He hadn't invited her into his domain from choice and was probably wondering how much longer it would be before she went.

She got to her feet and he turned his head slowly. 'What is it? Aren't you comfortable?'

'I must go,' she told him, ignoring the question.

It wasn't a case of not being comfortable—far from it. She was too comfortable for her own good out here in the velvet night, but she was tired as well and there was the drive back to Manchester ahead of her. They were all reasons to leave, but not the main one.

Adam's tetchiness at seeing her beside the marina had disappeared as he'd shown her around his domain. He'd been affable enough and once they'd gone back on deck he'd settled her in a chair and brought out a tray of drinks, but she'd sensed that politeness rather than pleasure had been behind it.

He didn't question her departure. He merely nodded and unfolded himself out of the chair, which brought to mind the comment he'd made when she'd told him that the male sex always saw her as fair game.

'You're quite safe with me,' he'd said, and it was clear that he'd meant it. Tonight had been proof and she ought to have been grateful, but perversely she wasn't. Not at this moment, anyway.

She turned swiftly, reaching out for the wooden rail beside the gangplank, but her chest seized up suddenly and she couldn't breathe. Lunging forward, she missed her hold and found herself sliding towards the water.

'Leonie!' she heard Adam cry in alarm, and then his hands came out, clutching at her beneath the armpits and pulling her back onto the deck.

As she lay looking up at him on the polished planking, he said hoarsely, 'What happened, for God's sake?'

She wasn't going to tell him that she'd just had another reminder that her health wasn't all it should be.

'I caught my heel in one of the cross-pieces of the gangplank, that's all,' she told him, raising herself shakily onto one elbow. 'I'm all right now.'

He was eyeing her anxiously. 'Are you sure that's what it was?'

'Yes. I'm sure.'

He reached down to help her up, and in assisting her to her feet Adam brought her close up against his chest, so close that she could feel the strong beat of his heart against her breasts.

'You've just scared the hell out of me,' he said as their eyes held. 'I thought I was going to have to fish you out of the water.'

'That makes two of us. Although I *can* swim.'

He wasn't listening. As if she hadn't spoken, he said, 'On a previous occasion I recall telling you that you'd be quite safe with me.'

Her eyes were challenging him. 'Yes, you did, and in

the light of you stopping me from slipping into the water it would seem that I am.'

'That isn't what I'm referring to, as you well know,' Adam said with his arms still around her. 'I'm talking about this…'

He took her lips gently at first and then with an increasing hungry urgency that brought her into a state of passionate response.

There was the smell of clean male sweat and tangy aftershave on him, and if she never got this close to him again the scent of him would live with her for ever.

Leonie's eyes were closed as the kiss went on and on. Her breasts, pressed hard up against him, were taut, her thighs aching, yet why did she feel that the moment had been spoiled?

Was it because Adam had reminded her of what he'd said, and on the heels of the reminder had come proof that he hadn't meant it, if this onslaught on her senses was anything to go by?

While she…she'd been wanting this from the moment she'd arrived at St Mark's. But how long had she been there? Not even a week. Hardly long enough to be getting into this state over a comparative stranger.

She didn't voice her thoughts but she might just as well have done for he released her suddenly, sending her staggering back, and said harshly, 'This is crazy. I've just done the very thing I promised not to, and breaking my word is something I'm not in the habit of doing.'

He raked his hands through the dark pelt of his hair. 'For one thing, we hardly know each other. For another, I'm happy with my life as it is…and, finally, I'm the last person to encourage relationships between hospital staff members, as it often leads to double trouble.'

'Points taken,' she told him with fatalistic calm. 'I shouldn't have come here. I'm sorry, Adam.'

He nodded grimly. 'Maybe that's the very reason you came.'

'Huh?'

'You don't like it when you're chatted up. But it appeals to you even less when someone comes along who isn't grovelling at your feet.'

'So you think I came here on an ego trip?'

'Did you?'

'No. I didn't. I came because…'

Her voice trailed away. What would he say if she told him the real reason for her invasion of his home—that because on the shortest of acquaintances she was in love with him and whether he wanted to make love to her or not nothing was going to change the way she felt?

Adam walked beside her without speaking to her car in the lane by the marina. He hadn't demanded she finish her explanation, so she concluded that he didn't want to know.

As the engine spluttered into life he did have one more thing to say, however. 'I hope that you're going to lock the doors and put the top up before you set off. If any of the late-night lager louts see that blonde mane of yours flying on the breeze, they might be inclined to give chase.'

'It's a quarter to ten, Adam,' Leonie pointed out levelly, 'and if I do attract some attention, at least I'll know what's in their minds—which is more than I can say for yours.

'I'll do as you ask because it's common sense but, please, don't assume that because you're my boss at work you have a say in my private life.'

Leonie's spirits couldn't have been lower as she drove home. The spherocytosis had reared its head two nights on the run for one thing, but worse than that had been the way the evening had ended, with the pair of them questioning each other's motives and Adam almost apologising for touching her.

What a fiasco! It would be a relief to get back on the

wards tomorrow, where reality was in plentiful supply and the kind of fantasies she'd been indulging in of recent days were a rare phenomenon.

Reality was definitely waiting for her on the paediatric unit the next morning in the form of a directive from a southern hospital to say that a heart had been found for little Alexandra Cottrell.

An ambulance was waiting to transfer the little girl to a hospital in Newcastle. At the same time as Alexandra was being taken there, an emergency flight was being organised to deliver the organ from where it had been donated.

Her parents were overjoyed and afraid simultaneously, and as Beth Carradine and her staff waved them off there wasn't a dry eye amongst them.

'How soon will we know if the transplant has been successful, Dr Marsden?' a young nurse asked of Leonie as she signed the discharge form for the child with the scalded leg.

'Soon. If not today, tomorrow. Organ transplants don't allow for any delay. Keep your fingers crossed for Alexandra. If it works she'll get a new lease of life, but if complications set in, well...'

It was late that evening before the news came through that the operation had gone ahead and it had been successful. After five and a half hours in Theatre the surgeon in Newcastle had been able to tell the child's parents that she was responding well, and by the time Leonie and the day staff arrived next morning there was even more cause for rejoicing, as the news was that Alexandra was breathing without the help of a ventilator and had regained consciousness.

* * *

As the weeks went by, Leonie had to accept that the evening she'd spent with Adam at the marina had set the pattern of their relationship.

They were friendly but guarded whenever they met in the corridors or in meetings that required her presence. It was often his deputy who stood in for him on the few occasions when she had to be present, and Mike Stacey, with his earnest but hardly invigorating approach to health care, was a poor substitute for Adam.

Adam's friendship with Joanne seemed to be flourishing and Leonie admitted to herself that she was jealous. But if ever she tried to broach the subject with her friend, with a view to discovering just how close the nursing manager was to the head of clinical services, she was met with either a blank stare or a quick change of subject.

The spherocytosis was still bothering her and a few times she'd had to excuse herself while on the ward or in Outpatients, but on the whole she was coping.

At least she was until the day that she was needed urgently on the unit and couldn't be found. Feeling breathless and nauseous, she had escaped into the hospital grounds for a breath of air, and it was while she was trying to overcome the lassitude that had assailed her that Adam came striding past.

'Derek Griffiths is asking for you,' he informed her. 'There's been an accident, involving a school bus. Some of the injured teenagers have been brought here and will be transferred to Paediatrics once they've been seen in Accident and Emergency. Is there a reason why you're out here?'

'Er, no,' she told him awkwardly. 'I was just having a rest.'

'You're tired?'

'No. I'll go right in.'

She knew that he was watching her as she went back

inside and that he wasn't happy with their brief exchange of words, but she wasn't sure of the reason.

'You always seem to be missing when I want you, Dr Marsden,' the senior consultant said tetchily when she got back to the ward. 'Please, keep yourself available in future.'

As Leonie went about her duties during the rest of the day she was considering what to do about her health problem. Whatever Derek Griffiths—or Adam—thought, she *was* pulling her weight at St Mark's and, apart from the odd incident, the spherocytosis wasn't affecting her efficiency.

It was unfortunate that she'd felt unwell at the very moment the senior consultant had required her presence, but she'd decided that it was better to remove herself from the ward for a few moments rather than flake out on the floor.

However, she owed it to Adam, in particular, to be frank about what was going on. She didn't want him to see her as a liability on his staff from a health point of view, neither did she want him to think that she wasn't taking the job seriously.

The next time there was a problem she would have to explain…and in the meantime there was plenty to do, with the children's wards overflowing with the intake of injured thirteen-year-olds from the school bus.

Adam had appeared a couple of times as the paediatric team took over from Accident and Emergency, and she heard Derek Griffiths complaining grumpily that he needed more beds.

'I've ordered a side ward to be opened up for the moment,' Adam told him, 'and in the long term, the bed situation and a reduction in waiting lists is my overall priority…as you well know, Derek, but I can't manufacture money out of thin air. I'll be bidding for extra cash at the next meeting of the trust board and you know that I don't accept a refusal to any proposals I make without a fight.'

The older man had dredged up a wintry smile. 'No. I know you don't, Adam.' He glanced around him at the array of plaster casts and cuts and bruises. 'I'd rather do a twelve-hour surgery stint any day than have your job.'

Leonie had been within hearing distance of the conversation between the two men and had been aware that Adam's dark gaze had switched to her as they'd talked.

As he was on the point of leaving he came across. 'Someone was asking for you in Reception as I came through,' he said coolly. 'Has anyone told you?'

'Er...no. I've only just surfaced from Casualty. I've been down there ever since the accident. I wonder who it can be?'

'You'd better go and find out, hadn't you? I thought it was probably this fellow you were waiting for in the gardens—a guy with a briefcase...about my age. Perhaps he wants to sell you something.'

He was turning to go but swung back again. 'Is everything all right with you, Leonie?'

'It would be if those I work with would stop jumping to conclusions about me,' she flared. 'Do you honestly think I would be skulking about in the hospital gardens, waiting for someone, when I'm supposed to be on duty?'

Answering spark with spark, he snapped back, 'So what *were* you doing out there, then?'

'That's my business!'

'And mine!'

'Yes, yours, too,' she agreed with sudden weariness, 'and you may find that all too soon I'll have to give you an explanation.'

'And what is that supposed to mean?'

She shook her head. 'Could we, please, leave it for now, Adam. If there's someone waiting to see me I'd better go and find out who it is.'

He nodded stiffly. 'Yes, do that.' And this time he went.

Leonie's eyes widened when the man seated in Reception looked up from the newspaper that he'd been reading.

'James!' she exclaimed. 'What are you doing here?'

'I'm here to see you, of course,' James Morgan said as his long face broke into a smile.

She was beaming back at him. 'That's very nice, but why?'

'I'm in Manchester for the day,' he explained. 'In fact, I'm due at the offices of the health authority in an hour, but first I thought I'd call to see you.'

Leonie perched on the seat beside him and as she did so he was eyeing her from beneath bushy brows. 'How's the spherocytosis?' he asked. 'I've been wondering how you're coping and if you've said anything to the management here. I've kept thinking that maybe I gave you bad advice when I told you to put thoughts of a spleen removal on hold.'

'It's not been too obvious so far,' she told him, 'but there are times when I feel very tired and breathless. I've found my niche here and love the job, which makes me anxious not to jeopardise it by having to keep sneaking off when I feel ill.'

'And that being so?'

'I think that in the near future I'm going to have to tell the clinical services manager about it as I've been getting frowned upon of late.'

'And what about the op? It could be beneficial, you know.'

'Yes, I'm aware of that, but it won't allow me to have healthy babies, will it?'

'Possibly not, but, Leonie, you need to think of yourself at this time in your life. Worry about babies when the time comes. You're not contemplating marriage in the near future, are you?'

'There was a time when I first came here that I had

yearnings in that direction, but they're fading by the minute.'

'And who's the lucky man? Another doctor?'

She shook her head and the long blonde plait swung gently to and fro. 'No. At least not in the medical sense.'

'And he's not falling over himself to do anything about it?'

'Not at the moment. We got off on the wrong foot.'

'Hmm. It does happen. But getting back to your rogue gene, I still think you'll be all right just as long as you don't pick up any chest or stomach infections. If you do, and there are problems, get back to me. Unless you'd prefer to be treated here?'

She reached out and squeezed his hand impulsively. 'Thanks for that, James. I would prefer to consult you, rather than everyone here knowing my affairs.'

'Are you sure you aren't referring to just the one person?' he asked quizzically, but she didn't take him up on it.

For one thing they'd only known each other casually at the hospital in Birmingham. James had been much higher up the ladder.

As he got up to go he said, 'What are you doing tonight? I wondered if you'd like to join me at the theatre.'

Her face brightened. It would make a pleasant change. If he hadn't already booked they could go to the Exchange. She'd been longing to go there ever since moving to Manchester.

'I'd love to,' she told him. 'And if I have a choice I'd like to go to the Exchange Theatre.'

The first person Leonie bumped into after he'd gone was Joanne. Her friend said teasingly, 'So who's the boyfriend?'

'James Morgan, a haematologist from the hospital in Birmingham where I worked before—and he's not my "boyfriend". He was passing and called in to see me.'

'What have you done to Adam these days?' Joanne asked with a swift change of subject.

'I haven't done anything. Why?'

'He isn't a happy man.'

'I know nothing about that.'

'Oh, no? You're the only person from this place who's seen the inside of the dream boat.'

Leonie stared at her. 'You're telling me that you haven't? I've always thought the two of you to be on the best of terms.'

'We are, but it hasn't run to that,' Joanne said laughingly. 'But, then, he knows I don't like being anywhere near water. I've told him that if he ever wants to make an honest woman of me he'll have to come and live at my house.'

'So it's possible that he might?'

'Everything is possible, my dear Leonie,' the nursing manager said with a wicked smile, and left her to ponder that as she made her way back to the wards.

CHAPTER FOUR

BRIEFLY putting to one side the hospital matters that constantly claimed his attention, Adam had followed Leonie to the reception area at a discreet distance, arriving in time to see the unpredictable Dr Marsden squeeze the stranger's hand affectionately.

So this wasn't one of the proposition merchants she'd complained of, he decided. Even if she hadn't touched the man he would have known that. There was an intimacy about the way they were conversing that spoke of something deeper, and Adam found himself breaking his own rules of conduct for a second time by showing an excessive interest in the private life of a fellow member of staff.

That evening on *The Apple* was still crystal clear in his mind because, to his complete mortification, he'd joined the throng of hangers-on that the beautiful Leonie was so wary of.

He must have been insane to have risked the frail rapport that had been springing up between them. Yet spoil it he had, and ever since she had been politely aloof.

But with the keen insight that was so much a part of his dealings with hospital staff, he sensed that there was something else adrift between them besides a clash of personalities, and he wasn't going to rest until he knew what it was.

As he walked thoughtfully back to his office he had a feeling that the man in Reception might have the answer. It could be simply a case of Leonie having found someone who wasn't just mesmerised by her looks and, having overheard him invite her to the theatre, Adam was sorely tempted to follow up the theory.

The Royal Exchange Theatre, rebuilt to high standards of elegance after the IRA's bombing of Manchester, was packed with an expectant audience who had come to see Richard Wilson in Samuel Beckett's *Waiting for Godot*.

Gazing around her with interest Leonie settled into the seat next to James on the first tier of the unique circular theatre and prepared to enjoy the unexpected evening out with a man who wanted nothing from her other than a good health report.

Her eyes widened. Two familiar figures were being shown to seats directly facing James and herself at the opposite side of the stage.

Adam and Joanne! What were they doing here? she wondered incredulously. Coincidence? Hardly! It was inconceivable that the two people who figured most in her life should decide to visit the theatre on the same night as James and herself.

The man at her side was following her glance and he asked, 'What's wrong? Seen a ghost?'

'Not exactly. But you see the couple who've just seated themselves facing us?'

'Yes.'

'That's my boss...and my best friend.'

James was eyeing them thoughtfully. 'I've seen him before. He went past when we were talking at St Mark's this afternoon.'

Leonie gaped at him. 'Really? I didn't see him.'

'Well, you wouldn't have. You had your back to him.'

So Adam had followed her when she'd gone to find out who'd been in Reception, she thought angrily. He took too much upon himself!

They'd been noticed. Joanne was waving and Adam was

permitting himself a cool nod in their direction. Her annoyance increased. Surely he wasn't checking up on her social life, as well as her performance on the job front? But if that were so, would he have dragged Joanne along?

Yes was the answer…if they were as chummy as she imagined them to be.

Well, they'd both get a piece of her mind tomorrow—Adam for snooping on her earlier in the day and continuing the process here tonight, and Joanne for going along with it.

As the lights were dimmed James said in a low voice, 'Am I right in thinking that he's the man you're interested in…and he's involved with someone else?'

'Yes. I think that describes it,' she said bleakly.

'So what's he doing here?'

'I don't know. Adam once said he'd like to visit this place, but it seems strange that we should both pick the same night.'

'Ours was a last-minute arrangement,' he reminded her. 'They could have had their tickets much longer.'

'Hmm,' she agreed dubiously.

James patted her hand consolingly. 'Forget about them, Leonie, and enjoy the show. They might be just as disconcerted at seeing us here.'

She thought not. Adam must have heard them make the arrangements and for some obscure reason of his own he'd made similar plans and brought Joanne along. And that was another thing she'd like to get to the bottom of. If those two were about to become a couple, or already were, why hadn't her friend said so?

The mere thought of Joanne sitting close to Adam in the darkened theatre made her feel lost and desolate. But she had no claim on him, had she? Adam was free to spend his spare time with whomever he chose—and his choice wasn't her.

For that matter it never had been. The only evening they'd ever been together had been as the result of manipulations on her part, and look what had happened to that!

Waiting for Godot was a finely produced and performed piece of theatre, but Leonie's mind wasn't on it. Every time she looked at the stage she was conscious of the dark blur opposite that was Adam Lockhart.

When at the end they filed out with the rest of the audience into the marble-pillared hall in which the theatre was housed, she knew with a fatalistic sort of resignation that Adam and Joanne would be waiting for them.

'Hi, there, Leonie,' Joanne said breezily, her eyes bright with curiosity as she observed the sandy-haired haematologist. 'Aren't you going to introduce us?'

'Of course,' she said coolly, acutely aware of Adam's thoughtful, dark gaze. 'I'd like you to meet Dr James Morgan. We worked in the same hospital before I came to St Mark's. James is in Manchester on business and took the trouble to look me up.'

As the two men shook hands Leonie said casually, 'And so what brings you here, Adam? It seems strange that we should all be here on the same night.'

Something glinted in his eyes at the question but she wasn't sure what it was—annoyance possibly, or amusement. It didn't matter. Just as long as he was aware that she knew he and Joanne weren't there by coincidence.

He shrugged as if the question were of little import. 'Yes, doesn't it? Joanne asked me round for a meal last week and in return I invited her to the theatre.'

Leonie eyed her friend. 'Must have been a rush for you to find a child-minder at such short notice,' she remarked innocently.

'No, not really,' the nursing manager replied. 'Adam had it all fixed up before he asked me. Jean Telfer is keeping her eye on my offspring.'

Leonie turned to face Adam again. 'Of course. A simple matter of providing a child-minder would be ''child's play'' to someone with your organising skills.'

The glint was there again in his enigmatic gaze, and this time it was clearly recognisable as ironic amusement.

'Correct,' he agreed blandly. 'Just as reserving a table at a nearby restaurant didn't tax my brain power too much. Would you both care to join us?'

'Not for me, I'm afraid,' James told him. 'I have to catch a very early train in the morning.'

'Nor me,' Joanne said. 'You should have warned me that we were eating out, Adam. I've told Jean I'd be back by eleven, and when I get in I've got school lunches to pack and clean uniforms to sort out.'

Leonie turned away as tears pricked behind her eyes. Would she ever have that privilege? Would the rogue gene that was affecting her life ever allow her to have children?

'Why don't *you* eat with Adam, Leonie?' her friend suggested. 'An early start in the morning is tugging at James and I've got my kids to see to. But nobody's pulling at your strings. You've nothing to rush home for and your place is only a matter of minutes away afterwards.'

Into the silence that followed Adam said easily, 'If that's how you feel, Joanne...and as long as Leonie is agreeable. But I'll take you home first.'

Joanne shook her head. 'There's no need. James and I can share a taxi. It can drop him off at his hotel first and then take me home.'

She turned to the only person who hadn't spoken. 'What do you say, Leonie? Will you stay and keep Adam company?'

With a feeling that she was being swept along by a current that was too strong to resist, Leonie fingered the fine gold chain at her throat and swallowed hard.

'I suppose so, if that would solve the problem.'

Her heart was thumping against her ribs. Dining with Adam might save him eating alone, but it would almost certainly create restraint between them.

Being alone with him had been the last thing she'd expected to happen at the start of this strange evening, and she was pretty sure that she was going to regret it, but how could she refuse the opportunity that Joanne had unwittingly, or so it seemed, thrown into her lap?

Fifteen minutes later the theatre crowds had gone and Leonie and Adam were left alone on the deserted pavement as the taxi disappeared.

'Keep in touch,' James had said meaningfully as it had drawn away and she'd nodded obediently, knowing that one day she would probably have to seek him out for the surgery that so far she had managed to avoid.

Adam was observing her silently, and with her earlier annoyance unabated she said coldly, 'You overheard James and me making our arrangements this afternoon, didn't you, and came to check up on me?'

He didn't attempt to deny it. Instead, he told her calmly, 'You weren't exactly whispering and, yes, I was curious about what you might be up to.'

If she'd been angry before, now she was furious. '"Might be up to"!' she cried into the summer night. 'If I'd intended spending the evening soliciting on a street corner it would still have had nothing to do with you!'

'Except for the fact that I'd have had to have you checked for HIV before I allowed you anywhere near my patients,' he said with continuing calm.

'Huh!' she snorted back. 'You see everything in terms of how it might affect St Mark's.'

'Maybe I do,' he agreed quietly, 'and, that being so, can I ask you a question?'

'Fire away. Though I don't promise to give you an answer.'

'Are you pregnant, Leonie?'

Her eyes widened in shock. 'What? How dare you ask me such a thing?'

It was Adam's turn to swallow hard. 'I'm asking you because sometimes you're positively glowing but on other occasions you look pale and ill, and if that's the reason I need to know so that allowances can be made for your condition with regard to your job.'

She turned away so that he wouldn't see the pain in her eyes. 'No. I'm not pregnant...nor ever likely to be. I, er, don't want children.'

It was a half-truth. Part of her was going to die at some future date when the subject came up with a man she wanted to marry, and the other part of her couldn't bear the thought of bringing children into the world who'd inherited a genetic blight from their mother.

Adam's face was white in the light of the streetlamps. 'That's a bit selfish, isn't it?'

She shrugged. 'Call it what you like. It's my body. My decision.' *And my nightmare*, she wanted to cry out.

His voice was completely flat as he changed the subject. 'Are we going to eat or not? I don't know about you, but I'm starving. I haven't had a bite since lunchtime.'

'Yes, if you like,' she agreed without enthusiasm. She was hungry, too. Or at least she had been until a few moments ago, but the conversation they'd just had had been enough to take away anyone's appetite.

Was he as concerned as this about all his staff? she wondered. Poking his nose into everyone else's affairs to the same extent?

As he studied the menu a few minutes later, Adam was telling himself that he was insane, not just for following

Leonie and her doctor friend to the theatre but for asking her such an intensely personal question.

Supposing her answer had been that yes, she was pregnant. What would he have done then? Made matters worse by asking who the father was? Questioning if it was the recently departed haematologist, for instance?

Yet the fellow had seemed happy enough to leave her in his company, just as Joanne had almost patted them on the head and given her blessing.

However, it wasn't the approval of those two he sought. It was a kind word from the beautiful woman who didn't want babies that he would appreciate, but he wasn't going about things the right way to get it.

For one thing, he'd used her physical well-being as an excuse to pry into her private life—he, Adam Lockhart, who kept his own personal affairs so separate from his job that those he worked with felt he showed hermit-like tendencies.

He looked up and her eyes were on him, bright blue pools of hurt and outrage, and he wished he could put the clock back to the winter night when they'd first met.

Across the table from him, Leonie was feeling more dazed than angry, had he but known it. Her annoyance had dwindled away with the realisation that she'd passed up the opportunity to explain about her illness when Adam had questioned her about her health.

Why, for goodness' sake, hadn't she grasped it with both hands and put him in the picture? She owed it to him. But it was the manner in which he'd brought the matter up that had stopped her confessing.

His unexpected appearance at the theatre had been a big enough surprise for one night, and to ask her if she was pregnant as a follow-up had really stunned her. It was the last thing under the sun she wanted to discuss with the only man she'd ever longed to have children with.

And now all she wanted to do was to eat the food that was being put in front of her and go home before the evening disintegrated any further.

It was about to take an upward curve. Adam was smiling as he said, 'Come on, Leonie. Cheer up. You may be working for a nosy, interfering workaholic, but I don't bite. In fact, some of my staff find me quite human.'

'Like Joanne, for instance?'

'Er, yes, I suppose so. We jog along amicably enough.'

'So you're not having a relationship?'

His head came up at that. 'Would it matter if we were?'

It was her turn to be asking personal questions, Leonie thought as she avoided meeting his eyes—and she hoped she could cope with the answers.

'From whose point of view?' she parried. 'The hospital's? Yours? Hers?'

'No. Yours, of course.'

'My point of view is different from most people's.'

'You mean because you're not gasping for the joys of parenthood? Lots of people get married and they don't all have children. Some just don't want them and others can't have them,' he said levelly, 'and how we've got on to this topic I really don't know. I merely asked whether you would have any problems if Joanne and I were a couple. After all, she is your best friend from all accounts.'

Would she have any problems? Was he kidding?

'No. Why should I? It isn't for me to say what you and she should do with your lives.'

'Just as you don't want me to interfere in yours?' he questioned softly.

'I didn't say that.'

'But it's what you think?'

Leonie sighed. They were going round in circles. Whatever had possessed her to agree to have supper with him?

She got to her feet. 'If it's all the same to you, Adam, I'd like to go. Thanks for the meal. I'll see you in the morning.'

He beckoned the waiter and grasped her arm as she made to leave.

'You surely don't think I'm going to let you walk alone through the streets at this hour!' he exploded. 'My car's parked close by, and as soon as I've paid the bill we'll go and find it.'

As she opened her mouth to protest he snapped, 'I know what you're thinking!'

'And what's that?'

'That I might be having an affair with Joanne but it isn't going to stop me trying my luck with her beautiful street-wise friend.'

'Streetwise!' she hissed angrily. 'I'm not afraid of being out late at night on my own, if that's what you mean, and it's a pity there aren't a few more women like me. So many cower indoors or use taxis, which turns the streets into stalking alleys for those of us who do venture out.'

If he was aware that she'd not taken him up on the rest of his observations, Adam didn't remark on it. Instead, he propelled her out into the night, and when they were outside on the pavement he said in a softer tone, 'Joanne and I are just good friends. What about you and the doc?'

As relief swept over her Leonie's face brightened. 'The same. I admire and respect James, but that's all.'

Adam let out a deep breath. 'And I'm not classed as just another opportunist after a beautiful woman?'

She was smiling now. 'What? The hermit of the Three Masts Marina? Hardly!'

He took her hand in his. 'As it's such a short distance I'll walk you home and come back for the car afterwards.'

'Mmm. I'd like that,' she murmured, and meant it.

The two of them walking hand in hand through

Manchester's heartland on a summer night, with some of their emotional cobwebs swept away, was a memory to cherish.

Maybe this was the right way to do it—getting to know Adam better, before putting the burden of her illness on him. It would be time to face up to its grim implications if ever she found that he loved her as much as she loved him, and he would have to care an awful lot to be prepared to forgo the joys of fatherhood.

But she was leaping ahead, taking it for granted that his blood warmed every time they were together, as hers did. She knew little about what made him happy. After losing his young wife so tragically, he might have found the contentment he sought in a solitary existence that he wouldn't want to give up.

'A penny for them?' he said quizzically as they strolled along King Street with its stylish paved walkways and elegant shops.

Leonie was thankful for the subdued light of the streetlamps that didn't betray her rising colour as she said casually, 'They're worth more than that, Adam. Much more.'

'But you're not going to tell me?'

Her laughter pealed out huskily. 'And make a fool of myself?'

Adam's grip on her hand tightened and he swung her round to face him.

'That's something we could both end up doing, Leonie, but at this moment does it matter? You're the most perfect woman I've ever seen, with your corn-coloured hair, those amazing blue eyes...and the other tempting gifts nature has blessed you with.'

He reached out and let a silken strand of her hair slide through his fingers. 'It seems incredible that you haven't been snatched up long ago.'

'I've been engaged twice and both times it was a disaster,' she said quietly. 'Lack of judgement on my part maybe, or short-sightedness on the part of my fiancés because they didn't expect me to have a brain underneath the packaging.'

'Then they were fools,' he murmured as he cupped her face between his hands. 'Blind fools.'

His kisses were sweet and wild, his arms like a heaven on earth, and as they melted together in passionate oblivion in the quiet street passers-by eyed the striking figure of the man and his beautiful companion with varying degrees of interest.

'I want to take you home and make love to you, Leonie,' he murmured at last against her smooth cheek. 'And not just because I lust after your body,' he teased softly.

She became still in his arms. She wanted it too, but... But what? She wasn't on the Pill because she'd seen no need for it with her recent celibate lifestyle...and Adam didn't seem like a man who carried condoms around with him as a regular thing.

He was reading her mind. 'What's wrong? Are you afraid that I might give you an unwanted child?'

The beautiful bubble which had held them was bursting as she took the escape he was offering.

'Yes. I am.'

It wasn't true, of course. She was afraid that he might give her a 'wanted' child, a child whose health would be at risk even before it was born. As another moment presented itself to come clean about the spherocytosis, she found herself still hesitating.

Only seconds ago Adam had described her as perfect. Could she be blamed for wanting him to hold onto the illusion for a little longer?

'Fair enough,' he said with flat finality. 'I'm beginning to wonder if your protestations about not being vain about your looks aren't a trifle overdone, as having babies can be an ageing and wearing process and lots of women sacrifice their youthful beauty while caring for them. Is that why you don't relish the thought, or do you just not like children? You were one yourself once.'

'My reasons are my own, Adam,' she said raggedly. 'I don't have to justify myself to you. My place is only a few yards away...I'll say goodnight.'

As she walked away from him she didn't look back, yet her ears were straining for the sound of hurrying footsteps behind or his voice calling her name. As she put her key in the lock Leonie knew that the evening which had been made up of both magic and misery was at an end.

If the long hours of the night were spent in restless questioning of the complexities of loving Adam Lockhart, there was no time to pursue them further the next morning.

For one thing, Leonie was nearly late arriving at St Mark's. She'd finally dozed off as a summer dawn had been breaking, and when the alarm had shrilled she'd turned over with a weary groan and ignored it.

When she'd eventually surfaced, the clock and her bathroom mirror had offered no comfort. One of them had informed her that she had overslept and the other had imparted the glad tidings that she'd looked like a washed-out ghost.

As she hurried towards the paediatric unit the thought uppermost in her mind was that she should give Derek Griffiths no further opportunity to find fault with her.

Beth eyed her sympathetically as she hurried into the office, fastening the buttons on her hospital coat as she did so.

'Traffic bad?' the ward sister enquired.

'No worse than usual,' she admitted. 'I overslept.' Casting a quick eye over the neat rows of beds outside, she queried, 'What's on the agenda for today, Sister?'

'Derek and one of the orthopaedic surgeons are doing a

shish kebab on Amy Taylor this afternoon,' Beth said. 'And
a fourteen-year-old West African boy has just come up
from Casualty with severe pains related to a flare-up of
sickle-cell anaemia.'

'Right. I'll see him first,' Leonie said as the familiar
routine brought normality to the day.

As Leonie bent over the boy's bed her earlier lassitude
had disappeared. The serious illness from which this child
was suffering came from the same group as her own, but
in this instance it was a form of haemolytic anaemia found
primarily in black people.

In his case it had been bequeathed to him by parents
both possessing haemoglobin S, an abnormal type of oxy-
gen-carrying pigment.

If only one of his parents had suffered from the abnor-
mality he would have inherited just the sickle-cell trait, and
would normally have been free of the dangerous symptoms
of the illness, but Jacob Motassi hadn't been that lucky and
an infection had brought about a sudden crisis.

He had been given an injection to stop the pain, which
was mainly in the bones, and a careful watch was being
kept on his kidney function as blood had been found in his
urine.

She was aware, as with her own illness, that the spleen
could be affected. In some young sufferers it had been
known to become enlarged, causing serious complications.

Leonie had seen children admitted to hospital before with
sickle-cell anaemia and usually, after careful nursing,
they'd been discharged, but only in the knowledge that they
might soon be back again, fighting the serious complications of a genetic problem that could eventually claim their
lives.

'How is the pain now, Jacob?' she asked gently as the
boy looked up at her in mute misery.

His eyes were huge in a smooth ebony face and they

were watching her lips. He's deaf, she thought in dismay. The disease had affected his hearing as it sometimes did.

'A bit better,' he mumbled, 'but it still hurts.'

'It will go eventually,' she soothed, mouthing the words as clearly as possible. 'The injection needs time to work. Can I get you a magazine? Or something nice to eat to take your mind off it?'

He managed a smile. 'Can I have a Mars Bar and a football magazine?'

'I'll see if that can be arranged,' she promised gently. As she turned away her own burden settled itself more firmly upon her slender shoulders.

Compared to sickle-cell anaemia, spherocytosis was a much lesser evil. She wasn't likely to die from it unless something very serious went amiss, but the effects of it could be most unpleasant.

So far she was coping. The attacks were relatively mild...but for how long?

As the busy day got under way there was no sign of Adam, and Leonie didn't know whether to be glad or sorry. The longing to see him again was strong, but what was there to say when she did?

Nothing perhaps. Too much had been said, disastrously, already. Yet the heady enchantment of the moments she'd spent in his arms had to be the measure of something.

They were two mature adults. Both of them were free to engage in whatever liaisons they chose and, for her part, if it hadn't been for the spectre of spherocytosis, she would have been on cloud nine.

Maybe she was making too big an issue of it. One thing was for sure—she'd gone the wrong way about telling him of her problem. Babbling on about not wanting children! If she'd started at the beginning and had mentioned the hereditary risks in the right context, Adam might have understood.

But would he still want her under those circumstances? He'd said nothing to indicate that he'd visualised anything other than a casual relationship and if that was the case...what was she worrying about, for goodness' sake?

'You look pale,' Joanne said teasingly as she seated herself across from Leonie in the staff restaurant at lunchtime. 'A late night, was it?'

'Not very. I was in bed by half past twelve.'

'How disappointing, after your friend James and I had made ourselves scarce.'

Leonie had to smile. 'It was all a bit sudden, wasn't it? I thought that Adam and you were more than just friends—until you buzzed off like you did.'

'And now that you know we're not?'

'Nothing.'

'Nothing! I guessed from the start that you were attracted to him and thought a bit of healthy competition might help things along. I know you have this hang-up about men only being interested in your looks, but Adam isn't like that—and it's time he started living again. He can't mourn for ever.'

'There's a reason why it wouldn't work out,' Leonie said tonelessly.

'What is it?'

'If he and I ever got to the point where we wanted to make a commitment, I wouldn't be able to give him children.'

Joanne was goggling at her. 'Why, for heaven's sake?'

'If I tell you, promise that it won't go any further?'

'I promise.'

When she had finished explaining, her friend eyed her sympathetically. 'That's awful, Leonie, but it's not the end of the world. Adam might not be bothered about fatherhood. It isn't your fault that you've got this problem.'

'No, it isn't,' she agreed sombrely, 'but what red-blooded male doesn't want to have children? I couldn't deny any man that.'

'And what about your function here at St Mark's?' Joanne enquired with equal solemnity. 'He ought to be told because of that, if nothing else.'

'Yes, I know. But in my own time, Joanne. I've got to pick the right moment.'

'I can see that. And you can rely on my discretion, but don't leave it too long. Adam isn't a man to be messed about, you know. A person with his organising skills doesn't like loose ends either here or in his private life.'

'Tell me about it!' Leonie groaned.

CHAPTER FIVE

As LEONIE thought about the forthcoming 'shish kebab' operation on the femur of little Amy Taylor's right leg, it seemed as if genetic illnesses were in abundance.

Osteogenesis imperfecta, commonly known as brittle-bone disease, was the cause of the many fractures the child had sustained so far in her young life, and because of their frequency her small body was becoming twisted and deformed.

Today, Derek Griffiths was going to operate to prevent further breakage of the femur by dividing the shaft of the bone into segments and skewering them onto a long intra-medullary nail that would keep them in a straight position, hence the term 'shish kebab'.

The surgery wouldn't prevent fractures in other parts of Amy's body, but at least it would give some relief to an area that seemed to be more susceptible than others. If this operation was successful, maybe there would be others that could help to make her life more livable.

Simon Harris was also aware of the implications of the operation and as they did the ward rounds Leonie said with a smile, 'What do you know about collagen, Simon? Our leader might just ask.'

He smiled back. 'I'm completely genned up on it. In Amy's case tests have shown it to be normal in quantity but deficient in quality, resulting in the whites of her eyes being bluish in colour.'

She patted him laughingly. 'Well done! And what is it?'
'What?'
'Collagen.'

'A tough, fibrous protein that holds the body cells and tissues together.'

'You'll go far if you keep this up.'

He grimaced. 'If I don't die from exhaustion first.'

A bustle behind them indicated that Mr Griffiths had arrived and the time for chit-chat was over.

'Have a word with Amy's parents, will you?' Derek Griffiths requested when the operation was completed. 'I have an appointment at the other side of the city in fifteen minutes with a private patient so I must dash. You can tell them that the operation was successful and that their little miss is in Recovery.'

Leonie nodded. She was quite capable of making the appropriate comments to the parents without being primed. But Mr Griffiths was pedantic and rather overbearing, and he had to put the words into her mouth before he went.

The Taylors were huddled together for comfort, their faces taut with misery, and her heart went out to them. They were never away from St Mark's for very long, and every trauma took its toll on them as much as it did on their small daughter.

Today's operation had been a correction rather than a repair and she was sure they were grateful that something was being done to try to improve the quality of Amy's life.

If the fair-haired, blue-eyed little girl had been born with the illness in its most serious form, she probably wouldn't have survived. As it was, the possibility that the broken bones would occur less frequently as she grew older did offer a small grain of comfort.

Her parents were aware of this, but at five years old there was a long way to go and in the meantime the greenstick fractures were a nightmare they all had to live with.

A restless night and the exertions of the day were taking

their own toll on her, but before she left for home Leonie stopped by Jacob Motassi's bed once more.

With the pain under control, the boy was asleep, his dark face gleaming on the starched white pillow. Beth and her staff would keep a careful watch on his progress, and at the slightest sign of any further complications an alarm would be triggered.

Leonie had just taken off her hospital coat and was about to sally forth into the early summer evening when she saw Adam's car glide into its parking spot outside the staffroom window.

Where had he been all day? she wondered. Certainly not in her vicinity. But his functions were many, the calls on his time endless. It was amazing that he'd found time to go to the theatre and with that thought the events of the previous night came crowding back to haunt her.

Dark-suited, with a crisp white shirt beneath, he was his usual immaculate self, but he wasn't swinging himself out of the car with his usual brisk grace.

Maybe she wasn't the only one who was feeling below par after a busy day, and that was a mild description of the pressures in the life of the clinical services manager. 'Gruelling' would be a better word.

If he was feeling jaded for once there was no sign of it when he appeared in the doorway behind her before she'd had time to gather her belongings together.

'Is that it?' he asked with chilly brevity. 'Finished for the day?'

'Yes, hopefully,' she replied in a similar tone. 'I was called back to emergencies twice last week as I was on the point of leaving, so I'm never really sure that I'm about to depart until I actually do.'

She dredged up a pale smile. 'And that's not a complaint. I'm merely passing a comment.'

Adam frowned. 'What was the reason? Short-staffed?'

'Simon Harris was ill. A gastric upset.'

'I see.'

'What sort of a day have you had?' she asked, the barrier still high between them.

He shrugged. 'Busy. Stressful. The usual thing. Keeping my finger on the pulse.'

'And now you're going home to *The Apple*?'

'Not yet. I've another meeting in half an hour.'

'Are you going to have time to eat before you go?'

There was surprise in his eyes. 'Er…no. I've got paperwork to deal with before I go.'

'What is the meeting for?'

'It's a disciplinary meeting, unfortunately. I hate having to sit in judgement.'

'I hadn't noticed. It didn't seem to upset you last night when you were holding forth on my shortcomings.'

As soon as the words were out she wanted to bite them back. They'd been having a pleasant enough conversation about the job and she'd steered it onto a personal level.

Adam's face tightened and chilly politeness was replaced with anger as he replied, 'You were the one who was bleating on about not wanting children. You didn't have to mention it. If you'd kept quiet I would have been none the wiser. Is it something you need to make clear to all your men friends before they get in too deep?'

'No! It isn't! I was merely being honest.'

'Yes, well, in future we'll keep our conversations strictly to St Mark's, the weather and other general chit-chat. That way we can't go wrong.'

I wouldn't count on it, Leonie thought dismally as he turned on his heel and left.

On her way out she had to pass the restaurant, and for once there was an appetising smell issuing through the door.

Popping her head round the door of the kitchen she asked one of the chefs, 'What's cooking?'

'Roast beef and Yorkshire pud…just out of the oven.'

'Sold,' she told him smilingly, and made her way to the counter.

'Two, please,' she told the girl, and hoped that she wasn't letting herself in for further aggravation with Adam.

Leaving her own meal on one of the tables, Leonie whizzed in the direction of Adam's office, holding the hot plate with a towel she'd borrowed from the counter staff.

Knocking with her free hand, she waited for the summons to enter. When it came and she entered, he looked at her in amazement.

'Leonie! What's this?'

'You can eat while you're working,' she said quickly, avoiding his eyes. 'Must go. I've left my meal in the canteen. I thought it would save us both cooking when we got home.'

He was eyeing the food. 'It looks delicious. Why not join me? Bring it in here?'

She shook her golden head. 'No, Adam. I don't want to disturb you.' As he opened his mouth to persist she closed the door behind her.

It was ridiculous, but as she ate in the almost deserted restaurant there was a glow of satisfaction inside her because Adam wasn't going hungry to his meeting, and when eventually he did return to the marina he wouldn't have to boil an egg or open a can.

How she knew that was what he'd do, she didn't know. But unless he was interested in cooking it was all that the average man would manage…unless there was a take-away nearby.

Driving home, the feeling of satisfaction was still there and all because she'd put a plate of food in front of a hungry executive.

'It doesn't take much to please you, Leonie Marsden,' she said out loud as she let herself into the silent apartment. 'The mother in you is showing, and that's the last thing Adam would expect of you.'

By ten o'clock she was feeling ill. Her head was aching and she was tired and breathless. After undressing listlessly, she was about to fall into bed when the phone rang.

'Leonie?' Adam's voice said at the other end when she picked it up.

'Yes?' she replied, trying to breathe some life into her voice.

'I'm on my way home from Bolton and in a phone box not far from your place. I wondered if I could cadge a coffee and at the same time thank you for looking after my well-being earlier this evening?'

She was swaying on her feet, bodily and mentally disfunctional. 'I'm just about to go to bed,' she informed him weakly.

'Why so early? It's only ten o'clock.'

'Yes, I know, but it's been a long day.'

Why she couldn't be truthful and tell him that she was too ill to see him, she didn't know, but how could she be sure he wouldn't make a fuss? Yank her in front of one of the consultants at St Mark's? He was entitled to.

Her reason for not saying anything was that if anybody was going to treat her, it would be James. Or maybe 'excuse' was a better word than 'reason'. The fact that she didn't want Adam to see her as anything less than whole had nothing to do with it…had it?

'So you can't wait up for another ten minutes?' he asked in disbelief.

When there was no answer, he went on angrily, 'You've got someone there, haven't you? Why not say so, instead of beating about the bush?'

'How did you guess?' she replied listlessly, and, without giving him further cause to complain, replaced the receiver.

As darkness fell over the marina Adam leaned back and closed his eyes. He'd been sitting out on deck, his long legs stretched out in front of him, ever since he got back, but tonight the solitude lacked comfort. He needed to hear a voice, one in particular, but there was only silence.

Apart from Leonie's kind gesture earlier, it had been a depressing evening. He'd had to sit and listen to a list of incompetences relating to a doctor whom he'd always admired and respected.

The fact that the incidents had been due to an only recently diagnosed mental illness, from which the doctor was suffering, hadn't raised Adam's spirits. The thought of the long-term repercussions to which the malpractices could lead to was a nightmare yet to be endured.

On his way home he'd deliberately driven in the direction of Leonie's apartment, desperate for someone to talk to—someone who would understand the pressures that such occurrences put upon him.

He mightn't have sought her out if it hadn't been for her kindness earlier, but she'd taken the trouble to bring him some food so she couldn't be completely averse to him.

At least that was what he'd thought, but she'd been so offhand when he'd phoned that it had been as if their relationship had taken one step forward and two steps back.

As the silver face of a summer moon looked down on him he got slowly to his feet. He loved *The Apple* and the peaceful stretch of waterway. It was like paradise. But in the Bible story there'd been three of them—Adam, Eve and the apple...and one of them was missing.

*   *   *

The following morning Joanne handed Leonie a brightly coloured envelope, and as she looked at it curiously, Joanne said, 'It's Rebecca's birthday the Sunday after next, and you're invited. I hope you're not on call.'

'No, I'm not,' she said, after reading the childish scrawl inside.

'Good,' Joanne said with a gratified smile. 'There's just one thing, though.'

'And what's that?'

'Adam will be there. He dotes on my two girls.'

She watched a shadow cross Leonie's face and said contritely, 'I'm sorry. I didn't mean to rub it in that he's fond of kids.'

Leonie swallowed hard. 'Of course you didn't, and, Joanne…'

'What?'

'I'm not so sensitive about my problem that I can't talk about children, or hear of someone else's fondness for them.' *Even if it is Adam*, her heart cried.

'Fine. Now that we've got that little problem out of the way, I'll go ahead with the arrangements,' Joanne stated with her usual breezy confidence.

'What's the format?' Leonie asked.

'It's to be a swimming party at the local baths, with eight small girls and us three adults to keep an eye on them.'

'Right. So it's swimming costumes and potted meat sandwiches, is it?'

'Something like that. Although these days the potted meat is likely to have been replaced with chicken nuggets. The local council, who're in charge of the baths, will be catering, so it's up to them what they provide.'

'Sounds a piece of cake,' Leonie said laughingly.

'Yeah. Birthday cake,' her friend remarked with a grin.

*   *   *

That had been a week ago and since then Jacob Motassi had been discharged in a happier state than when he'd been admitted, although the boy and his family and the staff on Paediatrics knew that he might soon be back. It wasn't a good prognosis but that was the way it was.

Amy Taylor had also been discharged, with at least one part of her small anatomy fracture-free, and at that moment her bed was occupied by a small boy who'd pushed a piece of Lego deep into his ear.

He was due to go to Theatre any moment to have it removed, and appeared to be quite unconcerned about the whole thing, which made dealing with him a lot easier than having to cope with a tearful or hysterical child.

On the lighter side of things, Beth was now sporting a modest engagement ring and, having seen how engrossed she and Simon were in each other, no one needed to look far for the prospective bridegroom.

Hospital romances happened all the time, Leonie thought pensively, and wondered how many of the female staff had set their caps at Adam.

However many it was, they hadn't been successful, and it was just her luck that when he'd turned his attention to her she'd had to pretend a lack of interest.

She'd felt much better the morning after she'd put him off when he'd wanted to call at her apartment, and had been reasonably well since. But she was never certain that it wouldn't change. A few times she'd been on the point of ringing James to ask for a further consultation about the removal of her spleen.

Adam was keeping his distance, treating her with cool politeness on the occasions when their paths crossed which wasn't often.

Yet on the day that Alexandra Cottrell's parents brought their small daughter in to see the staff of Paediatrics, he was just as delighted as the rest of them to see how well the child was progressing after her heart transplant.

Adam had been passing by when the family arrived on the ward and, on hearing the delighted exclamations, he popped in to see what it was all about.

'It's little Alexandra Cottrell, Mr Lockhart,' Beth told him. 'She was being treated at St Mark's when they rushed her off to Newcastle for a new heart. Isn't she gorgeous?'

'She is indeed,' he said smilingly as he slotted into one of the special moments in paediatric care when all those involved, in whatever sphere, rejoiced to see a very sick child restored to health.

Leonie was holding the toddler, with Alexandra's soft cheek against her own. As a chubby hand reached for the golden plait that swung on her shoulders Leonie laughed and the child gurgled in return.

When she looked up Adam's glance was on them and there was no frost in it. The dark eyes were warm and melting, his mouth tender, and Leonie felt tears prick in her own eyes.

This was what he strove for. What they all strove for. They were a team. Nothing else mattered, did it?

Yes, it did. It mattered that she couldn't risk having children of her own, though it wasn't the moment to be moping about that.

It mattered that Adam and she were going their separate ways when they could have been together. It mattered that...

He was moving towards them and when he came into Alexandra's line of vision the litle girl put out her arms to him. A cheer went up, and with the cool aplomb that was so much a part of him Adam reached out for her.

'This is how it could be, Leonie,' he said in a low voice so that only she heard him. 'Why don't you change your mind?'

*   *   *

She'd shared a table in the restaurant one day with Jean, and his willing slave had volunteered the information that Mike Stacey, Adam's characterless deputy, was moving on, and Adam was interviewing for the post.

'There's a very striking young lady in with him now,' Jean had said. 'She's highly qualified and they seemed to hit it off from the moment of meeting.'

Leonie's spirits had plummeted. 'Let's hope that she's a man-hater. Or married with a demanding brood to contend with,' she'd said, and as the elderly secretary had looked at her in puzzled surprise she'd got to her feet, saying as she did so, 'Don't mind me, Jean. I'm feeling down in the dumps.'

'You can write to Amanda Graves, informing her that she's got the position,' Adam said.

'I had a feeling she might have,' Jean remarked. 'A very attractive woman, I thought.'

'What? Attractive? Oh, yes, I suppose so,' he said distractedly, and she thought he seemed a bit odd. He was bending over the notes he'd made during the interview and he went on in the same manner, 'But it's not her looks I'm concerned with, Jean. It's her efficiency I'm bothered about.'

'Yes, of course,' she agreed, settling behind her word processor, and then, with Leonie's peculiar comment still puzzling her, added, 'Dr. Marsden said a strange thing the other day.'

She had his attention now. 'Who? Leonie Marsden?' His voice was rueful. 'She's turned it into an art.'

Jean sighed. Here was someone else who talked in riddles. 'I'm not with you.'

'Leonie Marsden is an artist when it comes to creating confusion.' He got to his feet and reached for his briefcase.

'I have more important things to think about now, like the meeting of the finance committee in five minutes.'

Two people whom she liked a lot weren't happy, Jean thought when he'd gone. They hadn't known each other long, but it seemed as if it had been time enough for them to have got off on the wrong foot.

It was Rebecca Archer's eighth birthday and when Leonie presented herself at the local baths where the child's party was to take place, she was met with the excited squeals of eight small girls arrayed in brightly coloured swimsuits.

'Have you brought your costume, Aunty Leo?' Rebecca's four-year-old sister, Tiffany, asked when she saw Leonie's slender figure framed in the doorway.

'Yes, I have,' she informed the tawny-haired little girl. 'I can't play games with you in the water without it, can I?'

'What's it like?' the birthday girl wanted to know.

'Just a plain black bikini.'

Joanne was having a last-minute chat with the organiser, and as Leonie looked around her she saw that one person was missing.

So where was he? The party had been due to start at four o'clock and it was ten past already. It wasn't like Adam to be late.

As she was squatting at the side of the pool, fixing armbands onto Tiffany, the padding of bare feet on the tiles came to a halt beside her. When she looked up Adam was standing beside them in a pair of dark blue bathing trunks.

'Hi, Uncle Adam,' the little girl cried and with safety precautions completed, she walked off to where her mother was waiting at the steps of the shallow end.

Leonie got slowly to her feet and her eyes met those of the man who was never out of her thoughts. They were both beautiful people—he tall, tanned and supple, with a fine covering of dark body hair, she wonderful in her blonde, semi-naked beauty.

On the face of it they were the perfect match, but inside...what? Confused? Wary? Frustrated?

'Hallo, there,' Adam said easily. 'I wouldn't have thought this was your scene. Joanne never mentioned that you were going to be here.'

'Otherwise you wouldn't have come?' she said with a smile that took the sting out of the words.

His dark brows rose. 'Rebecca is my god-daughter. It would take more than the world's most unpredictable woman to make me change my plans.'

'Or its most hard-to-understand man to make me change mine,' she riposted back with the smile still tugging at her mouth.

'Come on,' Joanne was calling from down below. 'We're going to start off with a race.'

As Leonie and Adam frolicked in the pool with Rebecca and her guests there were undercurrents in the water and they weren't from treacherous tides or steeply dropping ocean beds.

In Leonie's case they stemmed from uncertainty and longing. What was in Adam's mind she didn't know. On the face of it he was there merely to help the party along, but when they surfaced simultaneously, only inches apart, he reached out for her and drew her towards him.

'What are you doing afterwards?' he asked softly.

She was gasping, and not just because of being immersed in the water. 'Going home to recover.'

Adam was immediately tuned in. 'Are you all right, Leonie?'

'Mmm...yes,' she mumbled unconvincingly. 'Just a bit out of practice, that's all.'

He might be surrounded by water, with wet droplets glistening on his skin, but it was the bright, observant glance of the clinical manager of St Mark's that was looking her over.

Yet his voice was mild enough as he said, 'Why not go and help Joanne check on the goodies while I keep an eye on the party girls? We're going to play pass the parcel when we've eaten.'

'Waterproof-wrapped, I hope,' she said smilingly, as his brief show of concern warmed her heart.

Her friend was standing beside the buffet, gazing grim-faced into space, when she found her, and Leonie sensed trouble.

'Joanne! What's wrong?' she asked quickly.

'I've just had a message on my mobile to say that my mother has had a heart attack and has been rushed into Coronary Care.'

'Oh, dear! How bad is it?'

'Bad enough from the sound of it.'

'She lives in Devon, doesn't she…on her own?'

Joanne nodded sombrely. 'Yes, and I have to go to her, Leonie. I'd never forgive myself if anything happened to her and I wasn't there. But there are the girls. It's a long way to drag them with me and it will mean taking them out of school.'

They both knew there was an answer but it was left to Leonie to voice it.

'Leave them here,' she said. 'I'll come and stay at your place to look after them. Do they have one of those schemes for children to stay on a little while after school until they're picked up? If they do there's no problem. I can drop them off in the morning and pick them up on my way home at night.'

Joanne was nodding, already dealing with the pros and cons. 'Yes, they do. It's called Playlate.' Her voice broke. 'It would be marvellous if you could look after them for me, Leonie. You're the only person I'd trust them with…apart from Adam.

'I know he'll be only too willing to help, but for one thing *The Apple* isn't exactly geared to accommodating a couple of lively young girls, and for another he's a very busy man. Maybe you could join forces, though?'

'Yes, whatever,' Leonie said hurriedly, as the daunting prospect of the two of them playing at being parents reared its head. 'Just go, Joanne. It's a long drive.'

'I'll hang on for half an hour,' she said. 'The party's almost over, and when we get back home I can tell the girls what's happened in a calmer atmosphere and show you the ropes at the same time. Ask them to come and eat, will you?'

'What's going on?' Adam asked as they nibbled chicken nuggets and drank cola through straws. 'Joanne looks as if she's suddenly lost the party spirit.'

'She'll explain the first chance she gets,' Leonie told him in a low voice, 'and in the meantime it's happy faces for Rebecca's sake.'

Eventually the young guests had gone, and as Leonie took Joanne's daughters to help her wrap what was left of the birthday cake she saw their mother take Adam to one side.

What would he think of the hurriedly made arrangements? she wondered. She was about to find out, as his voice came over clearly through the open door of the next room.

'You're leaving them with Leonie!' he exclaimed. 'Don't you think that's…?'

His voice faded as the door was pushed to with a hasty click and she was spared from hearing the rest of his protestations.

So much for playing at Mum and Dad, she thought bleakly as she gathered up the debris from the party, but at least she wouldn't have him breathing down her neck while she was caring for the children. If the tone of his voice had been anything to go by, he would be keeping a watchful but disdainful distance.

Joanne had gone and there had been no tearful goodbyes. There had been sadness for their sick grandma, but the prospect of being left in Leonie's care had been a novelty that Rebecca and Tiffany were looking forward to and their mother's heavy heart had lightened at their easy acceptance of the new arrangements.

Adam hadn't gone back to the house with them, but he'd promised Joanne he'd look in later that evening. Having no wish to cause her friend further distress, Leonie had managed to restrain herself from telling him not to bother, but he'd observed her set face with a question in his eyes and she'd thought angrily how much she'd like to answer it.

But the chance would come. All that mattered at the moment were Joanne, her sick mother, and the two small girls. Her own life could be put on hold for a while until their needs had been seen to.

Enveloped in one of Joanne's plastic aprons, and unaware that she had a smudge of chocolate spread on her face, Leonie was involved in preparing the children's lunches for the following day when Adam arrived.

Rebecca had let him in and had then gone back to watch television. Oblivious of his arrival, Leonie was singing to herself as she worked.

'So. You've settled in all right by the look of it,' he said.

She swung round in surprise, her face straightening as the words of the song died on her lips.

'Yes,' she told him tartly. 'Does it surprise you?'

He looked good enough to eat in a smart black leisure shirt and grey trousers, with his hair shining from recent washing and the strong planes of his face for once relaxed.

While she…what did she look like? Her hair hung life-lessly as there'd been no time to wash the chlorine out of it or to repair her ravaged make-up…and what about the pinny?

A quick glance in a nearby mirror confirmed her worst fears—and if it hadn't, Adam was about to do it for her.

'Do you know you've got chocolate all over your face?' he was saying.

'That's war paint,' she told him acidly.

'And am I supposed to deduce something from that remark?'

'Yes, you are. You're supposed to realise that I heard your comments when Joanne told you I was looking after her children.'

'If that's the case, why are you annoyed? I don't remember saying anything derogatory,' he protested with irritating mildness.

'It wasn't what you said. It was the way you said it. Just because I'm not leaving a slot in my life for producing babies, it doesn't mean that I can't assume the role of motherhood if I have to!'

'You're getting steamed up over nothing,' he said as his jaw tightened. 'My lack of enthusiasm about you taking over here was because I feel that you have enough on your plate at the moment. The job is hard and demanding…and I have remarked that at times you look dreadful…'

'Thanks a bunch!'

'You know what I mean, Leonie, so don't be flippant. I just thought that maybe Joanne could have made other arrangements.'

'There wasn't time, Adam,' she said as her anger drained away, 'and I'm sorry if I misunderstood your comments. I was only too happy to offer my services in such a crisis…and don't worry. I'll cope. If you're concerned about

my performance at St Mark's, don't be. I'll take a course
of vitamins if I find myself flagging.'

She'd said it half-laughingly but now it was his turn to
be irate. 'For God's sake! You make me sound like some
whip-cracking slave-master, ready to sacrifice you on the
altar of my own demands! I am merely concerned about
your well-being—as I would be for any member of my
staff.'

Leonie turned away. If ever there'd been a time when it
wasn't right to tell him about the spherocytosis, this was
it. Adam really would have doubts about her capabilities if
he knew.

'And so I'm going to move in here with you,' he was
saying.

That brought her swinging back to face him. 'What?'

'I told Joanne I'd give you whatever help I could and I
can't do much if I'm miles away on *The Apple*. I'll go home
to pack a case and move into her spare room.'

'Right,' she agreed limply.

The 'happy families' bit was back on course with a ven-
geance and, caring for him as she did, there would probably
be more ups than downs to the arrangement.

If Joanne's daughters had been happy to have Leonie
looking after them, the addition of Uncle Adam to the
household was greeted with even more delight.

He had returned within the hour and now, scrubbed and
clean, Rebecca and Tiffany were on each side of him on
the sofa, snuggling up as they had their milk and biscuits,
before going to bed.

As Leonie observed them from the doorway there was a
lump in her throat. It would be easy to pretend that the girls
were his...his and hers. That they were a happy little family. But she wasn't going to allow herself to get into that
situation, was she?

Though would it matter all that much if her children did

inherit the spherocytosis? There was a fifty per cent chance that they might not...and the illness wasn't creating much havoc in her own life so far.

If she could come to terms with that line of reasoning there would be nothing to stop her from being her normal uncomplicated self with Adam. The love affair that they were on the brink of having could develop in the way that she longed for it to do.

It would be time to come clean about the illness if he ever asked her to marry him, but even as the thoughts took over her mind Leonie knew she couldn't do it. Not to him. Adam Lockhart, who liked all ends neatly tied.

She couldn't lead him on and then sweep the ground from under his feet. He deserved better than that.

CHAPTER SIX

AFTER Rebecca and Tiffany had gone to sleep, Leonie went into the kitchen and Adam followed, eyeing her questioningly as she stood, irresolute, in the middle of the floor.

'I think I should investigate the freezer and make some sort of a meal for us,' she suggested.

He shook his head. 'No. You've done enough for one day. I'll go and fetch some food in. There's an abundance of take-aways and fish-and-chip shops in the area. What would you like?'

'Anything. I don't mind. And thanks for the thought, Adam. It will give me the chance to have a quick shower while you're gone. My hair feels like rats' tails after being in the water.'

She was tired, too, not so much with the day's exertions as with its traumas, and her thoughts went out to Joanne, driving through the summer night to she knew not what.

The illness of Joanne's mother had caught Adam and herself up in the net of circumstance, and at this moment of truce she wasn't complaining. So far, all was going well.

The fact that for the next few nights they would be sleeping with just a wall between them was something she would have to adjust to when the time came.

Adam was picking up his car keys from the kitchen unit. 'I'll be off, then—and maybe by the time I get back you'll be ready to share some of the thoughts that are circling your mind. I can almost hear the wheels turning.'

He turned on his heel in the doorway and observed her with a half-smile. 'I suggest you put some plates to warm before you have your shower...and don't get dressed again for my sake, Leonie. You look as if you're the next one needing to be tucked up for the night.'

As she watched him walk down the garden path with the brisk grace that was so much Adam Lockhart, she wondered if he was volunteering to do for her what she'd done for the girls and tuck her up for the night in Joanne's bed. Or had it been just a figure of speech?

She might be feeling a bit frail, but a cosy evening with Adam was a more appetising thought than being bundled off to bed—unless it was to be a shared experience. And hadn't she decided that wasn't on the menu?

She would have liked him to have found her looking her best when he came back, but there was nothing for her to change into and the clothes she'd already worn were too crumpled to put on again without pressing.

Tomorrow she would go home and pack a bag, and in the meantime she would have to obey his instructions to some extent by not getting dressed again. An old towelling robe of Joanne's, which she'd rooted out of the airing cupboard, would have to suffice.

As she was drying herself after her shower the phone rang in the hallway down below. Draping the towel around her, Leonie went to answer it.

It was Joanne, sounding tired and anxious, ringing to say that she was at the Devon hospital where her mother had been taken and that her condition was serious but stable.

'How's everything at your end?' she wanted to know, and when Leonie explained that Adam had moved in with them there was a moment's surprised silence. Then, sounding more like her normal self, Joanne remarked, 'You see. The guy can't keep away from you.'

'It's you and yours that Adam's concerned about,' Leonie protested. 'He could be with me any time if he wanted.'

She heard the car pull up outside and went on to say, 'He's here now. Do you want to speak to him?'

'No,' her friend said. 'I have to get back to my mum. Give him my love and tell him thanks for helping out.'

Before Leonie could get back upstairs he was inside, a brown paper carrier bag in his hand and an expression on his face that told her food was the last thing on his mind at that moment.

'Joanne has just rung,' she said, acutely aware that she was displaying more than she was covering up.

'And?'

'Her mother is stable at the moment. She sends you her love and says thanks for your support.'

'Huh? Oh, yes,' he murmured absently, as the carrier dangled loosely from his fingers.

Leonie turned away quickly with escape in mind. When she'd rushed to answer the phone she hadn't planned a confrontation such as this—draped in a damp towel, with her face shining like a beacon and the golden glory of her hair plastered wetly against her scalp!

But he pulled her back with his free hand, dropping the carrier bag onto the carpet at the same time. The sudden movement released the towel from its loose knot, and before she could grasp its damp folds around her once more it fell at her feet.

Standing straight and still in her nakedness, she looked up at him, frozen by the unexpectedness of losing her towel.

'God!' he groaned as rose-tinted nipples sprang into hardness before his eyes. 'I've been content all this time without a woman in my life...and what has happened? The fates have presented me with a goddess!

'It's small wonder that the men you've known couldn't see any further than your physical beauty, Leonie. Working together as we do, *I'm* aware that there's more to you than just that, but at this moment I'm no different to the rest.'

'I desire you, too, Adam,' she breathed, throwing caution to the winds, 'and do you know why? It's because you *aren't* like the rest. You're like no one I've ever met before.'

She reached out and began to unbutton his shirt, aware that with every second their need for each other was gaining momentum. They were going to make love. It had been inevitable from the start. It was meant to be and she wasn't going to fight against it any more.

As Adam's hands went to the buckle of his belt the interruption that Leonie hadn't the will to create came from another source.

'Auntie Leo!' a tearful small voice called from the bedroom at the back of the house. 'I want Mummy!'

The would-be lovers froze, brought back from the edge of passion by another kind of need.

'It's Tiffany,' Leonie whispered. 'She's awake and it must have just sunk in that Joanne isn't here.'

Adam picked up the towel and wrapped it around her. 'Go to her. She needs you, poor little sausage. Talking of sausages, that's what's in the bag—sausage and mash. Something else that's cooling off through no fault of its own.'

With her foot on the bottom step of the stairs Leonie turned to face him, her face whiter than the towel. 'Maybe Tiffany's done us a favour, Adam.'

As his face hardened into incredulity she went hurriedly upwards to where the plaintive cry was echoing again, thinking as she did so that someone, somewhere, was watching over her...or were they?

Tiffany's cries had disturbed Rebecca and all three ended up in Joanne's bed, with Leonie in the middle and the children on each side, huddled close for comfort.

When Adam looked in later they were all asleep, and in the light of a bedside lamp he was concerned to see that the children weren't the only ones with tear-blotched cheeks.

He didn't flatter himself that Leonie had wept because she'd had to tear herself out of his arms—far from it. She'd seemed almost relieved that an excuse to break up the moment had presented itself.

So why had she wept? Not in sympathy with the children, surely. No. There was something in her life that wasn't right, and he would dearly like to know what it was.

He pulled the covers over them gently, turned out the light and then went to make up the bed in the spare room, thinking as he did so that *The Apple* and the tranquillity of the marina seemed a long way off—but for once he didn't mind.

Leonie awoke as the first light of day slid into the room. She was hot and had cramp in both arms, and didn't have to look far for the reason. There was a warm little limpet on either side of her.

At the same instant she became aware of the presence of the children, the events of the night before came back to her.

Adam! What must he have thought of her? Turning a moment of reassurance into a complete disappearing act!

She'd intended going back downstairs once the girls had settled to sleep again and, instead of carrying on where they'd left off, talking to him, telling him about the nightmare that was taking over her life. But by the time they'd calmed down her own eyelids had been drooping from sheer exhaustion, and that had been that.

It was only five o'clock but the sun was already promising a fine day ahead. Easing herself carefully out of the bed, she tiptoed along the landing.

The door to the spare room was shut and as she moved swiftly past it Leonie was already deciding that now was the opportunity for her to take the car to collect her belongings from the apartment.

If anyone should be around at that hour to question a tousled-haired blonde in an old towelling robe, driving a yellow sports car through the city centre, so be it.

She was back within the hour, to find silence still laying its mantle over the house. It was time to make up for the previous night's disarray, she thought thankfully.

By the time Adam surfaced she would be washed, dressed and combed to a standard that would hopefully blot out the memory of the wet waif of yesterday.

Leonie was standing over the cooker, taking boiled eggs out of the pan, and the children were seated at the kitchen table, happily spooning down their cereal, when Adam appeared in the doorway, already dressed for the stresses of Monday morning at St Mark's.

She was loth to look up and meet his eyes as there were unanswered questions between them from the night before, but thankfully when he spoke there was no rancour in his voice.

'Sleep well?' he asked, the question embracing them all.

Intent on their food, and with the insecurities of the night forgotten in the light of a new day, Rebecca and Tiffany nodded while Leonie, looking up at last, said quietly, 'I'm sorry I didn't do justice to the sausage and mash. I can't believe that I fell asleep.'

'But you're relieved that you did?' he countered.

'Yes...and...no.'

This wasn't the moment to discuss past embarrassments, she decided. Normality was required. 'Are you going to join us for breakfast?' she asked.

His eyes were on the clock. 'Yes, why not? I think I can manage coffee and a piece of toast.'

'And a couple of boiled eggs?'

'If that's what's on offer, yes. And then, if you'll make sure that the children have got all they need to take with them, I'll do the school run.

'It will save you being late and incurring the wrath of Derek Griffiths, as well as giving you time to prepare yourself for another busy day on the paediatric unit.'

Leonie smiled. This was harmony of the highest order. Happy families at top level.

'And will you pick them up after school?' Adam was continuing. 'I'm always bogged down at that time of day.'

'Yes, of course,' she agreed serenely.

All of this she could cope with. It was the limbo that she was left to wander in when it came to her love for him, and the price she would have to ask him to pay if ever she were to declare it, that defeated her.

'Does anyone know what's happened to the nursing manager?' Beth was asking of no one in particular as Leonie arrived on the ward that morning. 'I need to talk to her about staffing levels for the coming week.'

'Joanne is in Devon,' Leonie informed her. 'Her mother has been rushed into Coronary Care in one of the hospitals down there.'

The ward sister looked at her in concerned surprise. 'Oh, dear! What about the children? Has she taken them with her?'

'Er...no. I've moved in to take care of them while she's away. Adam Lockhart is aware of what's happened, so I imagine he'll be dealing with staffing requirements and so forth until Joanne gets back.'

There was no way she was going to tell Beth that she wasn't the only one who'd moved in to look after Rebecca and Tiffany. The hospital grapevine being what it was, they would find out soon enough, and that would give them something to talk about!

'We've got a couple of new admissions,' Simon said when Leonie went into the ward office to look over the weekend's reports. 'And Derek Griffiths has requested that you and I take over his clinic as he's been delayed.'

'So it's all systems go?'

'Looks like it,' he agreed.

One of the two children newly admitted to St. Mark's was suffering from acute gastroenteritis.

Six-month-old Kyle Baines had been brought into Casualty during the weekend by his eighteen-year-old mother, with the explanation that he'd had a bit of a tummy bug for the last couple of days.

On examination the child had shown all the signs of serious dehydration, and when questioned further his mother had admitted that the hollow-cheeked infant had suffered continual diarrhoea for forty-eight hours.

He'd been transferred to one of the paediatric wards and given immediate fluids, which had dramatically improved his condition.

Leonie checked his notes to make sure that only clear fluids with added glucose were being given to the child, and observed that tests on blood gases and stool cultures were being done.

As she was bending over the sick child with a staff nurse in attendance, a woman appeared at the other side of the bed. When Leonie looked up the woman said, 'I'm from Social Services. How is he, Doctor?'

'Much better, but there's still cause for concern. Kyle was a very sick child when he came here,' Leonie informed her, 'mostly due to him not being brought to us sooner.'

The newcomer sighed. 'Young, immature parents. Bad home environment. I could go on for ever. We've been concerned about him for some time and there's no way we can consider him going back home until he's completely well again. I shall ask that he be hospitalised for as long as possible, and in the meantime maybe we can find some better housing for the family.'

The other new patient was Philip, an eight-year-old who had been admitted that morning with a bout of recurring stomach pains. Over a period of eighteen months he had been complaining every now and again of discomfort in the centre and lower part of his stomach, and on occasions he had vomited.

Each time it had resulted in a couple of days off school before he'd felt fully recovered, and because the attacks were becoming more frequent, today his GP had sent for an ambulance when the young sufferer and his worried mother had presented themselves at his surgery.

When Leonie went to examine him his mother and a boisterous younger boy were hovering around his bed. As the pale-faced, nervous-looking child looked up at her pleadingly the thought came to mind that the boy's pain might be due to non-organic causes.

The mother looked to be a worried, fidgety type of woman, and when she volunteered that she'd suffered from a lot of undiagnosed stomach pains as a child, the idea took even firmer root.

As Leonie felt his taut little stomach there was nothing to indicate anything amiss, but she would nevertheless ask that a urine culture and barium tests be done.

'He's such a sensitive little soul,' the woman said. She gave a doting glance at the younger boy. 'Not a bit like young Sam here. He loves the limelight. Fit as a fiddle he is, too, which makes poor Philip seem even more sickly.'

As 'poor Philip' looked away, Leonie thought it might be worthwhile to point out that openly boasting about her younger son in Philip's hearing wasn't a good idea.

If Philip felt overshadowed by the ebullient Sam it could only make things worse. Another wise ploy would be to make light of his symptoms when the attacks came, instead of making a fuss.

When she got back to the office Adam was there, chatting to Beth and Simon, but the moment he saw her framed in the doorway he came over.

'Was everything all right when you got to school?' she asked in a low voice before he could get a word in.

'Not exactly,' he replied in a similar tone. 'Rebecca hadn't got her P.E. kit.'

'Oh! She never said she needed it!'

'Obviously.'

'So what did you do?'

'Went back for it, of course.'

'Which made you late getting here?'

'Correct.'

'I'll bet that was a first,' she said with a smile.

'Correct again,' he agreed blandly. 'And now I must go, having made my report to the house-mother, but first there's something I need to know.'

She was immediately wary. 'What is it?'

'When I looked in on the three of you last night the children weren't the only ones who'd been weeping. Why was that, Leonie? I don't imagine that your tears were for the same reason as theirs.'

Her colour had risen at the question. She'd wept for something she might never have as she'd held the two small bodies close, and now Adam was telling her that he'd walked in on them and seen the tear stains on her cheeks.

'It was nothing,' she said quickly, with a glance over her shoulder to make sure that the other staff weren't tuning in to their conversation. 'Just a moment of melancholy.'

She could tell Adam wasn't convinced but, given the

place and the time, he wasn't going to pursue it. His next comment confirmed it.

'I must dash. I've got a new deputy starting today so I need to be around for her.'

'Really? Your secretary told me last week that you were interviewing, but I didn't think you'd be appointing anyone so quickly.'

'The lady in question left her previous employment three months ago and since then has been resting, which means that she's free to start immediately. And it also lets Mike Stacey off the hook.'

'Jean said that you seemed very taken with one of the applicants. I believe ''striking'' was the word she used to describe her. Is it the same one?'

'Maybe. I don't know who she was referring to, do I?' he said with an edge to his voice. 'Her name is Amanda Graves. You'll be meeting her soon, no doubt.'

'No doubt,' Leonie repeated drily, and wondered why he couldn't have retained the services of the characterless Mike.

It was a week before Joanne felt that her mother was well enough for her to leave. Joanne would come home to make arrangements for her mother to move in with them, and her intention was to bring her mother straight to Manchester when she was discharged.

'It's the only way I'll be able to cope,' Joanne told Leonie during one of her regular nightly calls. 'If Mum goes back to her own home I'll be constantly worrying if she's all right, whereas if she's here with me and the girls I can see immediately if there's any cause for alarm.'

'And is she happy about the arrangement?'

'Moderately. She fancies the idea of seeing more of the children, but isn't over the moon about what she describes as giving up her independence,' her forthright daughter had to admit.

'How's it going with Adam?' she asked next, and there had been silence as Leonie debated her answer.

'Don't ask,' she said eventually. 'He's got a new deputy who's taking up all his time. They've worked late every night since she started.'

It was true. Adam had been there to do the school run each morning, but the time she'd hoped they might share in the evenings hadn't materialised because of his absorption with the dark-haired newcomer, Amanda Graves.

An extremely confident and immaculately turned out thirty-plus career-woman, Amanda was fitting into the deputy position like a hand in a glove, and it went without saying that she had Adam's approval.

That being so, why did they have to work so late? Leonie kept asking herself. She'd been in bed each night when he'd come in, and as she'd heard him go to his room she'd wanted to hurl herself at him and screech that this wasn't how she'd expected it to be.

Yet he was doing his share in other ways. When Tiffany had called out one night after a bad dream, Adam had been there beside her before Leonie had struggled into wakefulness, and twice he'd already had breakfast going by the time she'd come downstairs.

The knowledge that he was sleeping only feet away during the night was both comforting and frustrating, and as she alternated between sluggish sleep and wakefulness the memory of those fractured moments in the hallway on their first night of caring for the children was always there to haunt her.

Adam had never mentioned it since and she had to accept that there was no reason why he should. She'd made it clear as she'd gone upstairs to console the crying child that she'd been glad to be diverted from the love-making that had been about to take place. And, adding insult to injury, she'd ended up falling asleep, instead of going back down to be with him.

It was Friday night, and after a gruelling day on the wards Leonie was ready to fall into bed.

It had been a busy and tiring week but now, thankfully, it was the weekend and with some juggling of rotas she'd managed to avoid being on call, leaving her free to be with Rebecca and Tiffany until their mother arrived home late on Saturday afternoon.

The children were asleep and as on the previous nights there was no sign of Adam, which could only mean that the new deputy was still pulling his strings.

They'd been introduced briefly when Leonie had found them dining together in the staff restaurant, and even if she'd been bursting to like the new member of staff it wouldn't have been easy.

Amanda Graves had seemed like a coat of hard gloss paint against her own more malleable satin finish, and Leonie had thought bleakly that even the no-nonsense Joanne would have her work cut out dealing with this one.

She was halfway up the stairs when she heard Adam's key turn in the lock, and her grip on the bannister tightened.

'Hi,' he said in brief greeting as he closed the door behind him. 'Everything all right?'

It is now, she had the urge to say, and wanted to follow it up with a plaintive, I've missed you, Adam. But as it appeared that any yearnings he'd had in her direction had been put on hold with the advent of a more exciting candidate for his attentions, such a comment would have gone down like a lead balloon.

Instead, she replied coolly, 'Yes, of course. Why shouldn't it be?'

'No reason. Just that I haven't been around as much as I'd hoped to be. Anyway, we're off the hook tomorrow, aren't we? Joanne's back. That will be one problem solved, thank goodness.'

'But there are others?' she questioned, her voice still devoid of warmth. 'Such as how you put me back on my perch while you dally with the bird of plumage maybe?'

She took a deep breath. The comment had been short on dignity. If she didn't watch it she'd be on her knees, begging!

'Am I to presume that we're talking about Amanda Graves?' he asked with steely calm. 'Because, if we are, you need to understand that most of the time I've been showing her the job. And if there *are* some personal problems that she's confronted me with, I've been only too willing to help her sort them out—just as I would be for any member of staff.'

She supposed the rebuke was only to be expected. Adam was a free agent. He could transfer his attentions to whomever he liked, but there was something not quite right somewhere.

For one thing, his integrity was one of the things she loved him for. There was no greyness about him in either thought, word, or deed, so why—?

His voice broke into her thoughts. 'I'm going to make a coffee. Do you want one?'

'Have you eaten?' she queried.

'Mmm. We ate in the staff restaurant before leaving.'

'We?'

He sighed. 'Amanda and I.'

'I see.'

'I wish you did. I wish I did. At the moment my life is

in confusion,' he said flatly, 'and until I've come to grips with it, everything else is on hold. But once it's in order, you'll be the first to know.'

'Well, thank you, Adam,' she choked. 'That makes me feel so much better. But I won't hold my breath.'

'What's the matter with you?' he asked wearily. 'I thought I could count on you.'

'I'm a waiting-in-the-wings type, you mean?' She began to climb the stairs again. 'I'll give the coffee a miss if you don't mind. I'm going to bed.'

Leonie was back in the apartment, its tranquillity like balm to her wounded pride.

There had been a joyful reunion between Joanne and her daughters, with she and Adam presenting a smiling, united front, and now normality was taking over. The normality of living alone once more and facing up to the fact that she wasn't destined to be lucky in love.

Yet why bemoan the fact? You can't have it both ways, she told herself as she unpacked in the silent bedroom. If Adam had been falling at your feet, pleading for you to marry him or something similar, what would you have done? It still wouldn't have been right, would it, as then you'd be panicking about the dreaded spherocytosis? He's done you a favour, and the fact that he could change direction in just a week shows how much of an impact the glossy Amanda has made on him.

After Leonie had stormed off to bed the previous night, there had been no further sounds from below, and when she'd gone downstairs early that morning she'd found Adam asleep on the sofa, the dark shadow of bristles on his chin, his hair tousled and his tie slung over the back of the nearest chair.

Surely the human dynamo hadn't been so tired that he'd

flaked out before he could drag himself to bed? she'd thought. This thing he had going with Amanda must have some zest to it!

As she'd looked down at him her anger had started to diminish. Adam was entitled to be careful if he was contemplating another venture into marriage. He'd already had one raw deal through no fault of his own, and if he'd chosen her he would have had another sick woman in his life.

Her hand had gone out to stroke the dark hair, but it had faltered and the pain and disbelief had come crowding back as he'd sighed in his sleep and muttered, 'Amanda.'

And now she was back in reality, in her own place, doing as she pleased and enjoying it—except for one thing. It had started to hurt when she swallowed, there was a pricking at the back of her throat and her chest felt tight.

Thank goodness Adam wasn't around. She could suffer in solitude. In any case, antibiotics would do the trick. With regular and careful dosing she would have thrown off the infection that was taking hold and be well again by Monday morning. No one would be any the wiser.

Except that it was late on Saturday afternoon and the GPs' surgeries were all shut. The only answer would be to go to St Mark's and persuade someone to give her a prescription, but that would be bringing her health to the attention of others and some keen eye might just spot that it was more than a flu bug that she'd picked up.

'Steer clear of infections and you should be all right,' James Morgan had said, but the immunity that working in a hospital often created hadn't been strong enough to knock out the bugs that school children often brought home with them—and she'd bet that was where it had come from.

If she'd been in good health, no doubt she would have

fought it off, but in her present state she'd succumbed, and before she had a chance to decide whether to risk going to St Mark's for a prescription, she was feeling too ill to go anywhere other than to bed.

CHAPTER SEVEN

A PHONE call to the area's emergency services brought a young doctor to her apartment early that evening, and when Leonie explained the nature of her illness he was only too willing to prescribe the required antibiotics.

'There's an all-night chemist nearby,' he said, eyeing the feverish patient worriedly. 'Is there a neighbour or anyone who can pick up the prescription for you?'

Leonie shook her head. 'I don't know a soul in this place and my friends aren't so near that I could expect them to come chasing over at a minute's notice.'

Looking up at the concerned young medic, she thought that she must have a death wish. She knew perfectly well that Joanne would have been there in a flash if she'd known how ill she was, and so, Leonie hoped, would Adam, but her friend had only just got back from a week of trauma and had more to come—and Adam was the last person that she wanted to see her in this state.

The doctor sighed. The emergency control centre wouldn't be happy if they knew he was doing errands for the sick, as well as treating them, but he couldn't leave her to stagger out to collect her own medicine in the state she was in.

'I'll pick it up for you,' he offered, not quite clear in his mind if he was doing it because she was a stunning blonde or because she was merely a sick patient. But as he took himself off to the nearby chemist he consoled himself with the thought that, whatever the reason, it was the right thing to do.

* * *

By Monday morning the antibiotics were beginning to take effect, but Leonie felt so weak and ill that there was no way she was going to be well enough to turn up at St Mark's.

After a phone call to Personnel explaining the situation she went back to bed and lay gazing muzzily up at the ceiling.

When the visiting doctor had returned with her medication he had been undecided whether or not to have her admitted to hospital. If he'd insisted she would have gone along with it, so dreadful had she been feeling, but after some minutes' serious thought he'd decided that the antibiotics should do the trick and had eventually gone on his way, impressing on her that she must phone for him again if her condition worsened.

Fortunately it hadn't, but neither had she made a lightning recovery and as she lay amongst the tangled sheets the last thing she wanted to hear was the doorbell.

'Good grief!' Adam exclaimed when she opened the door to him. 'You look dreadful! How long have you been like this?'

'Since Saturday afternoon,' she croaked as she stepped back to let him in.

'What is it? A flu bug?' His voice had tightened and she knew that he was about to read her the riot act.

'Mmm, something of the sort.'

'And you've been alone all over the weekend...in this state?'

'Yes, apart from a very obliging young doctor who went to get my prescription for me.'

'Why didn't you send for me? Supposing you'd become worse?'

Little did he know that there'd been a strong possibility of that happening, with her immune system in the state it was, but she wasn't going to start going into details about that.

'Yes, I know,' she conceded, 'but I didn't, did I?' She dredged up a smile. 'Although there was a moment when I thought that I'd better put my insurance policies in a convenient place.'

'I suppose you think that's funny,' he snarled angrily. 'How do you think I feel? Knowing that you've been ill with no one to care for you?'

'It was just a flu bug, that's all,' she protested weakly, feeling that if she didn't get back to bed in the next few seconds she would end up on the floor.

He saw her sway on her feet and was immediately contrite.

'I'm sorry, Leonie. I should be looking after you, instead of lecturing you.' Swooping down, he lifted her effortlessly into his arms and said, 'Point me to the bedroom and we'll get you tucked up again.'

'You don't have to do this,' she protested as he laid her gently on the crumpled sheets. 'What about St Mark's? Surely there are lots of things needing your attention there.'

'I have a very efficient deputy. Or had you forgotten?'

She wasn't likely to have forgotten that.

'Amanda can cope for a few hours,' he informed her. 'And Jean is there to help if she has any problems. How long is it since you've eaten?'

'I can't remember. I think it was Saturday lunch at Joanne's.'

'That's forty-eight hours.'

'Mmm. It is, isn't it?'

'Have you any food in?'

She shook her head. 'No. I always do my supermarket shop on Saturday afternoons, but I'd started to feel ill by then and within an hour I was in no fit state.'

'I think the best plan would be for me to take you to *The Apple*. I can keep my eye on you there.'

'But you've only got one bedroom,' she wheezed.

'So? I can sleep on the sofa.'

'I can't let you do that.'

'Why not? There's no one else to look after you, is there?'

'No, but—'

'But nothing. That's what I'm going to do.'

He picked up her case, which was still lying where she'd left it after unpacking on her return from Joanne's, and said, 'I'll stick a few things in here for you, wrap you in a blanket…and carry you off.'

Leonie closed her eyes so that he wouldn't see how much the idea appealed to her. At that moment the complexities of their relationship were obscured by her need of him.

The thought of being taken under his brisk, caring wing was like paradise beckoning in her present state, and if anyone at St Mark's, including Amanda Graves, thought it strange that the clinical services manager was nursing a young doctor back to health and strength on his houseboat, they were welcome to do so.

Still huddled in the blanket that Adam had wrapped around her, and with a mug of hot, sweet tea in her hand, Leonie sat limply beside the placid waters of the marina as he swiftly changed the sheets on his bed.

This was the second week on the run that they'd been thrown together, she thought as a snowy white swan eyed her in graceful disdain from nearby.

First it had been Joanne's crisis and now she was in the middle of one of her own. If things had been different between Adam and herself she would have thought that the fates were smiling on them. But she had to remind herself that he'd brought her to the boat because it would be easier to keep an eye on her there, not because he was pining for her company.

She heard a footstep on the decking and then he was beside her, his shirtsleeves rolled up, a bundle of discarded bed sheets in his arms and the keen eyes that missed nothing looking her over with the authority of the self-appointed nurse.

Taking the empty mug from her hand, he nodded towards the stairs. 'Down you go, Leonie, and once you're in bed I'm going to warm up some soup for you.'

He smiled for the first time since bursting into her apartment. 'There's no one who can warm up a can of soup like yours truly, and then I'll have to leave you for a while as there are matters I must attend to at St Mark's. But I'll be back as soon as I can and, in the meantime, don't worry about a thing. Just try to get the soup down...and concentrate on getting well again. OK?'

She nodded mutely. If she tried to speak she would start bawling like a baby...and not just because she was ill. They would be tears of frustration and regret from the pent-up misery that came from the penance that she'd imposed upon herself.

If she hadn't loved Adam so much it would have been easy to captivate him. His deputy wouldn't have got a look in. There had never been any problems before in catching the eye of an attractive male, but in those instances there had been no deep feelings involved on her part, no need to fret over any wrong she might have been doing them.

But this was very different and as she went obediently down the narrow wooden staircase, with the blanket trailing behind her like a bridal train, Leonie was no nearer to knowing how to handle it than she had been before.

As Adam drove through the leafy lanes of Cheshire on his way to the red brick edifice of St Mark's in the centre of

Manchester, he was deep in thought. It was incredible that Leonie could have become so ill in such a short time. Yet it was so.

They'd left Joanne's house separately on the Saturday—he first, because he'd had some things to attend to at the office, while she had stayed on with Joanne for a while.

He hadn't been in touch with her over the weekend for two reasons. First, because he sensed a cooling off on her part and, second, because the arrival of Amanda Graves at St Mark's had put him in a quandary.

From having a life free of relationships with the opposite sex, he was now involved in two, and for once his crisp decisiveness wasn't pointing him in the right direction.

It was directing him to one course of action, though, and as soon as he got to the office he put a call through to the Birmingham hospital where James Morgan was based.

There was a limit to what he could ask the haematologist from an ethical point of view, but he was a friend of Leonie's and as such might be able to throw light on some of the things that had him puzzled.

'I'm sorry. Dr Morgan is away for the next two weeks,' his secretary said, and that was the end of that.

When he told Joanne, who was now back in harness until such time as her mother was fit to travel, her reaction to Leonie's illness made him feel once again that there was something he ought to know—and didn't.

'Where is she?' That was her first quickfire question.

'At my place now, but she'd been alone in her apartment all weekend.'

'Should she be hospitalised, do you think?' Joanne asked anxiously.

'What makes you say that when you haven't seen her?' Adam queried.

She looked away. 'I'm going on how you've described her condition.'

'Hmm. Well, according to what Leonie has to say for herself, she's better than she was, but she's staying put until I'm satisfied that she's on the way to recovery.'

'So you're going to nurse her back to health and strength?' Joanne asked with a teasing smile, her anxiety on hold momentarily.

'If I have to.'

The smile was still in evidence. 'If that's the case, half the female staff of St Mark's will be hoping to be struck down by a flu bug if it means there's a chance of recuperating on *The Apple*.'

'If that's all it is,' he said levelly.

'What do you mean?'

'I mean that I'm not totally convinced that it's just an influenza-type virus. She saw an emergency GP on Saturday, who prescribed antibiotics and told her to call him out again if she got any worse.'

'But as we both know, when they're called out at weekends under those circumstances it's more a matter of helping the patient to survive until Monday morning than going into any great detail over their condition. There are times when she doesn't look at all well and then the next time I see her she's fine. I know that life on the wards and in Theatre can be exhausting, but I do wonder...'

'Why don't you ask her, then?'

'What exactly?' he'd countered drily. 'If she's got galloping consumption? I can imagine her reaction if I start prying into her affairs. I'm not exactly her favourite person at the moment.'

'You ought to be. Scooping her up and carrying her off to your floating paradise.'

'Hmm. Well, that remains to be seen. I've been spending a lot of time with my new deputy during the last week.'

'And?'

'A situation has arisen that I wasn't expecting.'

'Such as?'

'You ask too many questions,' he said with a smile that didn't reach his eyes, and they went their separate ways.

Unaware that an in-depth discussion about her health was taking place, Leonie was sleeping in the big bed beside the portholes of *The Apple*.

The soup had gone down very well, followed by a glass of milk and a couple of biscuits. With the comforting feeling that she didn't have to cope alone any more, she turned her face into the pillow and slept for the first time since the infection had taken over.

When Adam returned in the early afternoon she was still in oblivion, and as he stood looking down at her he thought that even at her most defenceless she was undoubtedly the most beautiful woman he'd ever seen.

However, someone else was laying claim to his attentions. Amanda was asking for answers regarding a very new relationship and he had to get his thoughts clear on that before anything else.

It was evening when Leonie awoke and as she lay looking up at the planked ceiling of Adam's bedroom she was conscious of feeling better.

The medication was obviously beginning to take effect and that, along with knowledge that she was in Adam's care, had to be responsible for the improvement.

Reaching out for a hand mirror on the bedside cabinet, she allowed herself a quick scrutiny and groaned at what she saw. A white face with black smudges beneath the eyes, tangled hair and dry lips greeted her and, raising herself on her elbow, she reached for the blanket she'd been wrapped in during her transfer from the apartment.

But swift footsteps on the stairs made her pause, and when Adam appeared, bending as he came through the low arch of the doorway, she was lying back against the pillows once more.

'How are you?' he asked, taking her hand in his. He felt her pulse. She wanted to smile. Not content with having his finger on the pulse of St Mark's, now he was laying claim to hers.

'I feel better,' she said quietly. 'As if I'm over the worst of it. Adam...'

'Yes?'

'I really appreciate you bringing me here, but I don't want to be a nuisance.'

'You are a nuisance,' he said with a half-smile, 'but you'd be an even bigger pain if you were back at your own place and I was wondering all the time if you were all right.

'As soon as you feel up to it, you and I are going to have a nice long chat,' he went on. 'I think perhaps a visit to the medical staff's occupational health department is called for.'

'What? Just because I've had a dose of flu? No way!'

'Don't argue, Leonie,' he said firmly. 'If I say you're going, you're going!'

This isn't working out how I want it to, she thought miserably. If he sends me to Occupational Health my illness will be revealed and I don't want it to be like that. I want to tell him of my own free will...but not until I'm ready.

All I want at this moment is for Adam to know how happy I am to be here with him, in spite of whatever else is going on in his life. But we're ending up fighting.

'All right,' she conceded, holding back tears. 'If you want to play the big boss I'll do as you say. And now, if you don't mind, I'd like to get up and have a shower.'

'By all means, if you feel up to it,' he agreed in a milder tone. 'I'll make us a snack while you're having it. Leonie,

I don't know why me being bothered about your health should cause you such upset. Staff with health problems *are* my concern as they can affect the smooth running of the hospital.'

'Yes, I know,' she agreed wearily, 'and if ever I feel that I'm about to become a passenger, you'll be the first to know.'

In fact, there was now no reason why she shouldn't tell him about the spherocytosis. Adam was involved with someone else so, fool that she was, there was no need to worry about depriving him of children as their relationship wasn't going anywhere, was it?

As she came out of the shower Leonie could hear voices up on deck and she froze. He had a visitor. Maybe it was Joanne, although she hoped her friend would stay away for the time being as she didn't want to pass on the infection to her and the children.

But it wasn't Joanne's breezy tones she could hear up above. The voice was deeper and vaguely familiar, and what it was saying kept her rooted to the spot.

'I need to know, Adam. I can't go on like this. You have to make a decision.'

'I have done, Amanda,' he replied. 'There's only one person I need to speak to and once I've told her and got it off my chest, so to speak, there's no reason why we can't come out in the open about our relationship.'

'And how do you think she'll respond?' his deputy asked tightly.

'It doesn't matter, does it? All that counts is that I will have done the honourable thing on behalf of us both.'

'And suppose I lose my job?'

'Don't concern yourself about that. There'll always be another slot somewhere in the health service for you.'

'Maybe,' Amanda Graves said flatly, 'but I want to be near you.'

'The feeling is mutual,' he said with a warmth that turned Leonie's blood to ice. 'Meeting you has been one of the most amazing things that has ever happened to me. Nothing can change that.'

'So when are you going to tell her?'

'Tomorrow. Or as soon as the opportunity arises,' he promised.

'You're a darling,' the husky-voiced visitor said, and in the silence that followed the sound of high heels on the gangplank proclaimed her departure.

'Hi,' he said easily when Leonie appeared on deck, this time in a sweatshirt and linen trousers that she'd found in the case he'd hurriedly packed for her.

'I've just had a visitor—Amanda Graves.'

'Yes. I heard her. Having me here must have made it awkward.'

He was frying bacon on the small stove, and at the comment he whirled round to face her.

'Why?'

'Why?' she repeated angrily. 'You were discussing me and I was only a few feet away.'

'Your name wasn't mentioned.'

'Not in so many words maybe.'

Adam switched off the gas tap and, pointing to the nearest chair, said soberly, 'Sit down, Leonie. We need to get something straight. If I've been preoccupied with Amanda—and, God knows, I have—it's been for a very good reason. You know how obsessed I am with everything being above board that I'm involved in?'

'I thought I did.'

'I don't know what you mean by that, but I am.'

'And?'

'Over the last week I've been in a great predicament.'

'You're saying that you haven't been able to decide which of us you fancied?'

'Don't be ridiculous. I'm serious.'

'So am I.'

He ignored that. 'Shortly after she came to work at St Mark's, Amanda and I discovered through casual conversation that we are half-brother and -sister. It was a mind-boggling revelation, not least because I had employed a close relative on my staff, which is strictly against hospital protocol.'

Leonie was goggling at him, slack-jawed. 'So you're not in love with her?'

'No, of course not. I'm overjoyed to know that I have a sister but that's all.'

She was still dumbfounded. 'And you never knew she existed?'

Adam shook his head. 'No. My mother left us when I was small and I was brought up by my father and my grandmother. I never knew what had happened to her, but apparently she'd been living not many miles away, had remarried and given birth to a daughter.'

'So now you have the opportunity to be reunited with her,' she said gently, visualising the pain that the small boy must have endured at the loss of his mother's love.

His face was sombre. 'Sadly, no. Amanda tells me that she died last year.'

'And so who is it that you have to discuss this with?'

'The only person I'm answerable to in the trust—Mary Challenor, the chief executive. I'm going to have to tell her that I've inadvertently employed my half-sister in my department. It will depend on what she says whether Amanda stays or goes.'

He was eyeing her regretfully. 'So you can see why I've been so preoccupied over the last week.'

'And you couldn't have told me?'

'Not with someone else involved—in this case, my sister. I had to speak to Mary Challenor first and she isn't due back from holiday until tomorrow.'

'I thought it was a case of love at first sight,' Leonie said awkwardly. 'You must think me a complete idiot.'

'Never that,' he said with a dry smile. 'Secretive maybe, or too independent, which could affect your thought processes to some extent, but not to the degree of idiocy.'

'Why are you accusing me of being secretive?' she asked slowly as his words sank in.

He'd turned the gas back on and the bacon was starting to sizzle in the pan.

'Oh, come on, Leonie!' he growled protestingly. 'Don't insult my intelligence. I've been dealing with hospital staff for a long time and I can smell it a mile off when someone isn't being straight with me.'

'So you think I'm deceitful?'

She was playing for time and knew it, but she needed to gather her wits. The incredible news that Amanda was Adam's half-sister had completely staggered her, but there was exquisite relief in knowing that was what she was—his sister.

But where did that leave her? Still in the position of being in love with a man who would almost certainly want children if he ever remarried? She'd seen him with Joanne's little girls and it had been as clear as daylight that he would make an excellent father.

But the man was no fool. He'd sensed that she wasn't being truthful, and if there were any recurrences of the infection she would have no choice but to tell him.

His voice was breaking into her harassed reasoning.

'Don't put words into my mouth, Leonie. The word I used was ''secretive'' which as we both know has a completely different meaning to the word ''deceitful''.'

He dished out the food he'd prepared and beckoned her to the table.

'Come and eat…if you feel up to coping with my very basic culinary skills. Then perhaps you'd like to sit out on deck for a while. It's a beautiful summer evening out there. Not a night to be wasted on niggling and confusion.'

She sighed. Adam was right. It wasn't a night to be wasted, but there wasn't a lot she could do about that on the heels of an infectious bug which she would hate to pass on to him *and* the code of conduct she'd set herself, dictating a low-key presence on her part in any case.

As they watched the sun go down on the skyline, seated side by side, there was brief contentment in her. They were together. It was better to live for the day than the lifetime, and when Adam reached out and took her hand in his her grip tightened on the strong fingers entwined in hers.

'What?' he asked curiously.

She shook her head. 'Nothing. I love this place and I'm just happy to be here.'

His eyes darkened. 'With me?'

'Of course. That's what it's all about…being here with you.'

Should she tell him that she'd ached with jealousy when she'd thought he was attracted to Amanda? No. That might create a confrontation and she hadn't the strength for any more word battles.

'If you were in a less frail state I might take you up on that kind remark,' he said smilingly, 'but nurses aren't supposed to seduce their patients.'

'Spoken like a true clinical services manager,' she parried laughingly, grateful that the rush of colour his words had brought to her cheeks was being absorbed in the rosy glow of the setting sun.

She got to her feet. The conversation wasn't going to lead anywhere because *she* wasn't well and *he*...what was he? Uninformed?

'What's wrong?' he asked. 'Have you had enough?'

'Yes. I'm tired.'

She was, but not of him. Never that!

He had risen to stand beside her, concern in his eyes. 'I want you to stay here until you're fully recovered. There's no way you're going back to your apartment until then. Agreed?'

'If you say so.'

'I do. Now, off to bed with you. I'll give you a shout when I'm leaving in the morning.'

As she undressed Leonie's smile was pensive. This could have been such a romantic interlude, just the two of them in the peaceful backwater. Instead, Adam would have his nose to the grindstone at St Mark's and she...what would she be doing? Taking the tablets!

It was Leonie's fourth day on the boat and she was beginning to feel that she'd lazed around long enough.

Adam had set off for London very early that morning, along with two other members of the trust, to take formal acceptance of some government funding which had been promised, and would be very late back.

It promised to be a long, empty day and, with the return of some of her vitality, she decided to attack some household chores.

In the middle of the morning the phone rang, and her face creased in surprise when James Morgan's voice came over the line.

'James!' she exclaimed. 'What can I do for you? And
how did you know I was here?'

'It's what I can do for you, Leonie,' he said, 'and your
friend Joanne told me how to find you.'

'Joanne?'

'Yes. I wanted a word with you and rang St Mark's, but
they told me you were off sick and it was then that I started
to put two and two together. When there was no reply from
your apartment I got back to the hospital and had a word
with her, and here I am.'

'I'm not with you, James.'

'That's not surprising. I'll put you in the picture. I'm on
holiday at the moment. Decorating my flat of all things. I
rang my office on some minor matter earlier today and my
secretary mentioned that someone called Adam Lockhart
had been trying to get in touch with me.

'Now, I don't know what you think, but I immediately
thought of two reasons why he would do that. Either you
were seriously ill and he was letting me know, me being a
friend of yours. Or he was checking up on you.'

'I have been ill,' she said slowly, 'but not so seriously
that they've had to give me the last rites. That leaves your
other suggestion and that's quite believable as Adam
guesses that I'm keeping something back.' Her voice rose
at the hurt of it. 'But what a nerve, to try to pump you for
information!'

'If your diagnosis had come through before you left
Birmingham the need wouldn't have arisen,' James said
evenly. 'The medical staff's occupational health department
at St Mark's would have seen that you have spherocytosis
from the records that we passed on to them. But because
you had the tests under my jurisdiction, and didn't get the
result until you'd moved, you slipped through the system

However, what's this about you having been ill? What was the problem?'

'I picked up a virus which knocked me for six. I managed to get antibiotics and I'm now recovering, but at the time I was so ill it was scary. Adam called to see me and bundled me back here to his houseboat so that he could keep an eye on me. But it sounds as if he's been doing more than that. The cheek of the man!'

'It's his job, Leonie,' he reminded her, 'and he's entitled to know that sort of thing. Although it goes without saying that I would never abuse a patient's confidentiality...even though that patient is a doctor.'

'I'd like a further consultation with you, James,' she said flatly. 'When can you fit me in?'

'I'm back a week on Monday. How about then? My first appointment before I tackle the backlog?'

'Fine. I'll book a day's leave...and once I've seen you I'll tell Adam.'

'You're considering the op, then?'

'I thought that maybe you could run some further tests and from the results advise me what to do.'

'By all means. I'm concerned about you and I'm still not convinced that I gave you the right advice in the beginning. Now, Leonie, if you'll excuse me, I'll get back to my paper-hanging.'

She'd been calm enough as they'd ended the conversation but now, alone on *The Apple*, she was despairing. If Adam was so desperate to pry into her affairs why hadn't he spoken to the employees' occupational health at St Mark's? Although, she thought with a grim smile, it wouldn't have done him any good if he had.

As James had just pointed out, the details of her illness would have slipped through the system as she'd changed jobs when she had, but at least Adam would have been within his rights to have done that. Checking her out through her friends was outrageous!

He could keep his Cheshire idyll, she thought painfully. She would rather be in her apartment, alone and uncared for, than with someone who went behind her back.

It was almost midnight when the phone rang and even though she'd been braced for it ever since going back home, Leonie still found herself tensing.

'So that's where you are!' Adam's voice said accusingly when she picked it up. 'You never mentioned anything about leaving when I was setting off for London this morning.'

'That's because I wasn't thinking along those lines then,' she informed him, 'but since then I've had James Morgan on the phone and discovered that you'd been trying to get in touch with him.'

There was silence at the other end of the line, and with a chill in her voice she went on, 'Am I right in assuming that it was something to do with me, as it was only through me that you made his acquaintance?'

'Yes. It was in connection with you that I wanted to speak to him,' he said levelly.

'Checking up on me, weren't you?'

'Not in the truest sense of the word. I was merely going to ask him if there was anything I should know with regard to your physical fitness. It would have been up to him whether he enlightened me.'

'I can't believe that you would do that, Adam,' she flared. 'Why didn't you ask me, instead of going behind my back?'

'If you remember, I already *have* done. I brought up the subject the other day and you evaded the issue, as you've done on other occasions, so don't start saying that you're being persecuted—you're not. I'm concerned about your welfare, that's all.'

'And the smooth running of St Mark's?'

'Yes, that, too...and why not?'

'Why not, indeed, but in future will you, please, stay out of my affairs? I'm an intelligent adult and as such I'm quite capable of managing my own life.' And on that note she rang off.

CHAPTER EIGHT

ON THE Friday morning Leonie rang the hospital to tell Joanne that she was back home.

'Why, for heaven's sake?' the nursing manager asked. 'The girls and I were intending to visit you over the weekend. They were looking forward to seeing Uncle Adam's boat.'

Leonie sighed. 'I'm sorry about that Joanne, but I *am* back in Manchester.'

'For what reason?'

'I'm almost well again.'

'The truth, please, Leonie.'

'Adam has been checking up on me with James and we've had words.'

'Ah! That would explain why he turned up this morning looking like a man who's lost a pound and found a penny. Though he did perk up a bit after being closeted with Mary Challenor for half an hour.'

'That's good,' Leonie said. 'She must have accepted his explanation.'

'About what?'

'He'll tell you when he's ready.'

'I doubt it. He's gone back to frowning again.'

'I'm hoping to be back on Monday,' she said, switching the conversation into more mundane channels.

'And so what are you going to put on your ''self certificate''?' Joanne wanted to know. 'Not spherocytosis, I'll be bound.'

'No. I'm not. It will just state that I've had flu. But I think I shall have the operation, Joanne. I should have had my spleen removed when I first found out what was wrong with me. I let myself be swayed by the fact that I'd only just started at St Mark's and didn't want to have anyone doubting the contribution I could make on the paediatric unit.

'But by delaying it I've created a situation that's awkward to say the least. I wanted Adam to see me as a whole woman, for what good that has done me, as I'm never likely to be that, am I?'

'You're too hard on yourself,' Joanne protested. 'It isn't your fault that you've been lumbered with a faulty gene. You're not the first and you won't be the last. It happens to lots of people. No one knows that better than those of us who work in a medical environment. Supposing it was the other way round—that Adam could pass on something unpleasant to any children he might have and wasn't prepared to risk it. How would you feel?'

'I would accept it, rather than face the rest of my life without him.'

'There you are, then!' Joanne proclaimed triumphantly. 'You have your answer. If *he* doesn't feel the same when you tell him, he isn't worth his salt.'

'You make it all sound so simple,' Leonie told her wryly. 'He's got to want to marry me first.'

'And does this rapport that he has with his new deputy make you have doubts about that?'

'No. He's explained what has been going on between them and it's something rather wonderful and totally unexpected that's happened, but it's not for me to tell you. He'll want to do it himself.'

'Now you've made me curious. So, if he hasn't fallen for the glamorous Amanda, why do you think he doesn't want you? If you're right, he'll be the first man ever who wasn't falling over himself to carry you off to his castle— or, in this instance, his boat.'

Leonie's laughter was mirthless. 'Thanks for the vote of confidence but, for one thing, Adam isn't impressed with my general behaviour. He thinks I'm deceitful and it isn't the pull of another woman that will end up keeping us apart.'

'I hope you're not inferring it's a man!' Joanne countered jokingly.

'No. It's an organisation—St Mark's Hospital. That's all he cares about.'

'Oops! Here he comes…with the gloom still very much in evidence,' Joanne said at the other end of the line. 'Will speak to you again. And Leonie, you're wrong about him.'

On the journey back from London on the Thursday night Adam had been anticipating the pleasure of finding Leonie waiting for him on *The Apple*.

If she wasn't asleep she would almost certainly be in bed by the time he arrived, he'd thought, but just the mere fact of knowing that he hadn't been returning to an empty boat had given him a warm feeling.

It was strange that it had never bothered him in the past, but he'd supposed that it all depended on who was waiting for him—and Leonie Marsden was a sight for sore eyes at the best of times.

He wouldn't have known she'd gone if the bedroom door hadn't been wide open, but the message from that had been loud and clear. She'd left. Where she'd gone he hadn't known, but it had been pretty clear that if she'd left *The Apple* the obvious place for her to have gone had been back home.

The frosty conversation he'd had with her at midnight had wiped out the last dregs of his anticipation and he'd gone to bed with his mind awash with a mixture of anger and frustration.

Leonie was right to be annoyed at him ringing James

Morgan, he supposed, but, damn it all, he'd done it with the best intentions. Why in heaven's name did she have to be so prickly?

He arrived at St Mark's in a sombre mood the following morning but his meeting with Mary Challenor lightened his spirits. The senior executive of the trust told him smilingly, 'I have no problems with your half-sister being employed in your department, Adam. I have complete faith in your integrity and believe you when you say that you had no idea who Amanda Graves was when you offered her the position.

'Obviously you think she's the right one for the job so let her get on with it, and if there are any comments when your relationship to her becomes common knowledge, refer them to me.'

He left her office thinking it was good to know that somebody thought he could be trusted and he went to tell Amanda the good news.

'Let's go out tonight to celebrate both things!' she said. 'Finding each other…and me keeping the job.'

'Why not?' he agreed.

At least something was working out right, and for the rest of the day he put thoughts of Leonie firmly to the back of his mind.

It turned out to be the second miserable weekend on the run for Leonie as she did a delayed shop for food and for the rest of the time moped around the apartment. The only good thing was that she was feeling better physically than the week before.

Joanne wanted to bring Rebecca and Tiffany round to see her but Leonie persuaded her not to. 'Just to be on the safe side,' she said. 'However it ended up, it was a flu-type virus I had in the first instance, and the last thing you need at the moment is for either yourself or the girls to catch it from me.'

Her friend groaned into the receiver. 'That's true enough. Mum is arriving tomorrow and she, of all people, needs to be kept free of infection. She's being transported from Devon by ambulance, so for the next few days it's going to be all systems go.'

By the time Monday morning came Leonie was eager to get back to St Mark's. Since she'd last spoken to Joanne her condition had improved greatly and she felt that she was going to be able to cope once back in harness.

The fact that by returning to work she was going to be in Adam's orbit again was a thought she pushed away every time it intruded.

With plenty of time to think during the last few days, she'd admitted to herself that she'd made a great fuss over what he'd done to try to justify her own actions. When one was in the wrong it was tempting to shift the blame onto someone else, thereby hoping to detract from the original fault, and that was what she'd done.

But it didn't change anything. An abject apology wouldn't alter the main issue. The operation she was now prepared to undergo would improve her health immensely, but it wouldn't make her a good bet as a wife and mother.

It was better to leave matters how they stood.

They were doing the ward rounds, Simon and herself, when Derek Griffiths appeared.

'So you're back with us, Dr Marsden?' the taciturn senior consultant said when he saw her.

Was that doubt in his voice? Leonie wondered. Was he someone else who had a suspicion that she might be a creaking gate? Not from a dose of flu, surely.

No, she decided. It was his normal brusque manner, which, fortunately, he kept for his staff. His attitude towards their small patients couldn't be faulted. He was kind and patient, but was rarely seen to make them laugh, while she and Simon went to any lengths to bring a smile to a pale little face.

The face of the two-year-old girl who had just been admitted was anything but pale. It had the flush of a high temperature, with lips that were sore and cracked and eyes with the bloodshot look of conjunctivitis.

'Do you have any thoughts on this one?' Derek asked as the three doctors hovered around the bed. 'Temperature persisting for over a week and what looks like a measles-type rash starting to appear, along with other symptoms.'

'I've seen something like it once before,' Leonie said with a comforting smile for the little sufferer, 'and if it's the same thing it's inflammation of the blood vessels that's the root cause. Kawasaki disease?'

The elderly paediatric consultant nodded approvingly. 'In medical terms, mucocutaneous lymph node syndrome.' He reached out and felt the little girl's neck. 'Hence the swollen lymph glands. Feel for yourselves.'

As the other two doctors followed suit he turned to Sister Beth. 'This is a tricky one, Sister. The illness is quite rare and usually only attacks pre-school children. All we can give the child is intravenous immunoglobulin and aspirin to reduce any damage to inflamed arteries.

'Usually it's a one-off and most children make a complete recovery, but while the illness is at its most severe there can be heart damage if the coronary arteries become seriously inflamed.'

'Are we going to tell the parents that?' she asked. 'They've probably never heard of the illness.'

'No. I don't suppose they have. It gets its name from an outbreak in Japan over thirty years ago, and, yes, I think that we have to explain the complications that might arise.

'But the GP was pretty prompt in getting her to us, and if the aspirin dosage is commenced immediately the outcome looks hopeful. Obviously, I'll arrange for tests to be done.'

He looked around him. 'Where are the parents?'

'The mother has had to dash back home to see other children off to school and the father is serving in the regular army. He's being contacted,' the ward sister informed him.

'Right. Well, when they show up you can explain what we're dealing with, Dr Marsden. Never let it be said we kept them in the dark. And well done, picking up on the Kawasaki disease.'

It was good to be back, she thought as they moved on to the next bed, if only to receive the grudging approval of Derek Griffiths.

But there was someone whose approval meant more to her than his, and her face warmed when she saw him moving towards them with his purposeful stride.

They'd been bound to meet sooner or later in the hospital confines but Leonie wished it hadn't happened while she was in the company of the other two doctors.

She needn't have worried as Adam immediately made it clear that anything he had to say to her wasn't for their ears.

'Can I borrow Dr Marsden for a moment, Derek?' he asked smoothly. 'I won't keep her long. Just a couple of things I want to discuss with her.'

Derek smiled. If there was one person he did approve of at St Mark's it was the clinical services manager. Adam Lockhart was a man after his own heart. Clever, practical, fair, and a glutton for punishment when it came to the hard slog of running all the various services that went to make St Mark's one of the top hospitals in the north.

'Yes. Carry on,' he agreed amicably. 'I'm sure that Dr Harris will be able to provide any answers I might need.'

As Leonie watched Simon's face redden she gave him a conspiratorial wink, and in tones as smooth as the ones

Adam had used said, 'I'm at your service, Mr Lockhart. Where is this discussion to take place?'

'My office,' he said flatly, and led the way out of the ward without looking back to check that she was following.

Resisting the impulse to let him find that she'd gone elsewhere, she followed him at a leisurely pace, and by the time he reached the door of his office she was only just turning the corner of the corridor.

'If that's the fastest you're capable of, maybe you'd have been better having another week off,' he said when she finally caught up.

'It isn't the fastest I'm capable of,' she said coolly. 'I just don't have any intention of scuttling along at your heels like a lap dog.'

Adam gave an angry snort. 'That'll be the day!'

He motioned for her to go in, and she sailed past him with all the grace of the slender, long-legged creature that she was.

His mouth twisted and she thought she saw misery in his eyes, but his voice was as confident as ever as he said, 'First of all, how are you? Are you better?'

'Yes, I'm fine.'

It was a lie. Getting up, showering, making a quick breakfast and driving to work—it had seemed an effort and there was the rest of the day to get through, which was making her think that possibly she wasn't as well as she'd thought she was.

'So you're in sparkling form?'

'I didn't say that.'

'Because it would be a lie?'

'Is this what you've brought me here for?' she flared. 'To try and catch me out?'

'No, it isn't. I'm having a small dinner party on *The Apple* on Saturday night to celebrate the discovery that I have a sister. Amanda is bringing the man that she lives with, Derek and his wife are invited, and Joanne is bringing Philip Scott, the fellow who's just bought the house next to hers.'

'What about her mother and the children?'

'Her mum is pottering about now and Joanne will see the girls in bed before she comes.'

'And so what has all this got to do with me?'

'I'd like you to be there, too.'

'What? Are you sure?' Before he could reply she went on, 'Ah. I see. You can't find anyone else at such short notice.'

'It isn't short notice,' he said through gritted teeth. 'Amanda and I decided on it last week, but I've been waiting until you were well enough to be there. What is it with you, Leonie? All this bile because I made a simple phone call to your friend, James Morgan.'

'I'm sorry, Adam,' she said contritely, as remorse swept over her. 'I made a big thing out of nothing. Thanks for the invitation. I'd love to come.'

That's if I'm still on my feet after being back at work for a week, she felt like adding, but she'd told him she was fine and so anything other than a gala performance wouldn't do.

'So we're friends again?' he asked, his expression lightening.

'Yes, why not?'

She could cope with being friends. It was when the chemistry between them started heating up that she began to panic.

Her eyes took in his trim outline in the smart suit and it was easy to imagine lean flanks, a hard chest and all the other parts of him that could set her on fire if she let them.

A black jacket with cropped trousers to match and a sleeveless white silk vest underneath it, extra make-up to hide her pallor, and the thick swathe of her swept-back hair in golden braids—these all made a statement, Leonie thought as she inspected herself in the mirror before leaving the apartment on Saturday night.

Exactly what the statement was, she wasn't quite sure. Perhaps she was anxious to show Adam just how good she could look, for all the time she'd been recuperating on *The Apple* she'd looked like death warmed up.

Or maybe it was for her own benefit, to give her extra confidence now that they were back on a more friendly footing after her apology.

Whatever it was, she hoped that Adam would be suitably impressed.

He was.

'You're the first to arrive and you look stunning, Dr Marsden,' he said as she came up the gangplank. 'If I remember rightly, the last time you came to visit you were wrapped in a blanket.'

Caught up in the pleasure of the moment, she smiled across at him, her weariness forgotten. 'Don't remind me, Adam.'

She was on deck beside him now. 'Although on second thoughts maybe you should.'

'What?'

'Remind me.'

'Why, for goodness' sake?'

'Because I've been incredibly rude. I never thanked you for looking after me. I went off in a huff without telling you how much I appreciated you taking the trouble to take care of me, but I'm going to make up for it now.'

She leaned across and kissed him gently on the cheek. 'Thank you for looking after me, Adam.'

As her lips touched his cheek he became still, but only for a split second, and then he was swivelling round so fast that before she could move away he had her in the circle of his arms.

Looking down into her startled face, he said softly, 'It was a pleasure, Leonie, just as this is going to be.'

As her lips parted in surprise his mouth came down on hers, and as they melted together Leonie knew that they could never be just friends. The attraction between them was too strong.

His touch was like magic. The clean male smell of him was like a heady perfume, his lithe grace a constant stimulant to the senses. And it wasn't only his body that held her in thrall. His mind was just as captivating. She wanted to spend the rest of her life with this man, and for a brief, reckless moment she allowed herself to forget that nothing was ever that simple.

They were standing hip to hip. His hands were in the hollow of her back, holding her with a sort of triumphant possessiveness that made her senses swim.

There was no way it would have stopped there if they'd been alone, but voices on the bank brought them back to the real world and with a groan he released her and stepped out of the shadows slanting across the deck.

Derek and his wife were making their way on board, and Adam said in a low voice, 'Don't leave when the party's over, Leonie. We have some unfinished business.'

They did indeed, she thought bleakly as he went to greet his guests, and that was how it was likely to stay—unfinished.

There was none of the super-efficient career-woman about Amanda tonight, Leonie noted. Her face was softer, her eyes less hard. She was obviously very happy to have found the brother she hadn't known existed, and Adam in turn was making it clear that he was equally delighted to have found her.

Her partner, a pleasant, heavily built man called Roger

Blair, who was in computer sales, said to Leonie at one point in the evening, 'It's a small world, isn't it? Amanda didn't even know her mother had been married before, but a chance remark and Adam's keen eye, spotting her mother's maiden name on her application form, took them into an unbelievable set of circumstances that have changed their lives.'

He glanced across to where Amanda was smiling up at Adam. 'She's over the moon to have found him.' Eyeing Leonie good-humouredly, he said, 'If you and he are a couple we might be seeing quite a lot of each other in the future.'

'We're just colleagues,' she said quickly. 'I'm here to make up the numbers.'

He laughed. 'I can't believe that. Not after seeing the way Adam looks at you.'

'You have to, I'm afraid,' she said quietly. And so does he, she vowed silently.

As Leonie surveyed the limited accommodation on the houseboat it was clear that there were no signs of food being prepared, and when she caught Adam looking at her questioningly she said, 'I can't smell anything cooking.'

'You won't,' he said, his dark eyes warm with the memory of their earlier bonding. 'I'm having it brought in. The caterers should be here any minute. If you remember, my only cooking accomplishments are with the can opener or the frying-pan at its most basic.'

Before she could reply Derek had joined them, commenting casually that Adam would be lucky to get away with having a close relative working for him.

'I've already explained to Mary Challenor that I had no idea who Amanda was when I engaged her, and she has no problems with that,' Adam said in a cooler tone than he usually used when addressing the senior consultant.

Leonie hid a smile. Derek might be top man on Paediatrics, but he wasn't going to be allowed to patronise Adam.

'How do you like my new neighbour?' Joanne asked in a low voice after Leonie had been introduced to the man at her side.

'He seems all right,' she said doubtfully. 'Just how friendly are you?'

'What's that supposed to mean?' her friend hissed.

'Exactly what it sounds like,' Leonie told her levelly.

'We're just getting to know each other. Does that satisfy you?'

'I wasn't meaning to be tactless,' Leonie said quietly, 'but if you're intending to introduce another man into the children's lives you should give it a lot of thought.'

'Thank you, Dr Marsden,' Joanne said with heavy irony. 'I'll bear it in mind.' Then, with a forgiving squeeze, she added, 'You're right, of course.'

The food was excellent and the company congenial, and as Leonie looked around her the thought came that it was a night for new beginnings, the most important one being that of Adam and his half-sister. Hopefully, their lives would be enriched by the relationship.

Then there was Joanne with her new neighbour. He seemed a nice enough fellow and was seemingly undaunted that the woman at his side had in her life two children from a previous marriage.

With regard to herself, the future didn't look quite so rosy. She wasn't going to obey Adam's instructions to stay behind, much as she would like to. Common sense told her that was the pathway to heartbreak.

The guests were ready to leave, and when she joined them on deck his dark brows drew together, but he didn't say anything. He just wished her a curt goodnight and left her to follow the others onto the canal bank.

He'd got the message, Leonie thought glumly. And if

James Morgan said what she expected him to say on Monday, she would be even more out of favour with Adam when she informed him that she was going to have to take more time off.

As she drove away with a quick wave for the rest of the party and a swift parting glance at *The Apple* it would have been a comforting thought if the spleen operation would mean the end of her problems.

Healthwise, it might be, but she still wouldn't be sure of producing healthy children. Nothing was going to change that.

James had repeated some of the tests he'd done previously while Leonie was in Birmingham on Monday, but he was pretty sure that nothing would have changed.

'In this type of anaemia the problem is caused by the red blood cells being demolished more quickly than the bone marrow can produce them,' he said. 'This is due to the fragility of their outer covering.

'The only way to improve the patient's general health is to remove the spleen, which is the main site of the destruction. If you decide to have that done you'll feel much better in the long run, but you'll still have to keep clear of infections as much as possible. You've had the pneumonia jab, haven't you?'

She nodded, grappling with the implications of what he was saying. It was obvious that she was going to have the operation done. It was the sensible thing to do, not only for her own well-being but so that she would be less of a liability in her job.

With regard to Adam's place in the scheme of things, she wasn't as clear. If he knew she was having the operation he'd be entitled to know why, and when he found out, what would his reaction be?

He would want to know all the details of the illness, and

what then? Would he feel that he'd had a lucky escape? Be dubious about her future usefulness in his beloved hospital?

Supposing he were never to find out? That she had it done without his knowledge and came back fighting fit to take up where she'd left off? But where had she left off? The chemistry was there between them in no uncertain terms. Could she keep him at arm's length for ever? There was no choice. She would have to.

Why not just tell the man? a voice inside her said. Let him make his own decisions. It's your own vanity that's the problem.

Maybe it was. Or maybe it was the thought of rejection that she couldn't cope with.

'Are you going to have the surgery done privately, or come in here as an NHS patient?' James asked.

She frowned. That was a tricky question. She was a doctor, working for the NHS, and all her instincts said that was how she should be treated. But this hospital would send the bill for her treatment to St Mark's, and if Adam saw it and knew nothing of what had been going on then her secret would be out.

It was a risk she would have to take. For one thing, to have the surgery done privately would take every penny of her savings and, she thought with a grim smile, she didn't want to end up as a pauper as well as everything else.

'I want to come here,' she told him.

'Very well. I'll set it up, but it could be a few weeks before we can fit you in.'

'That's all right. Just as long as I can keep telling myself that the decision has been made.'

'And what about Adam Lockhart?' he wanted to know.

'What he doesn't know about, he won't concern himself with,' she said airily, and wished that James looked as if he believed her.

*   *   *

'Where were you yesterday?' Adam asked abruptly when they came face to face on the hospital car park on Tuesday morning.

'I took a day's leave,' she informed him, visualising his expression were she to explain why.

'I see. Any particular reason?'

'I went to see a friend to arrange a holiday.'

That had to be a first—a stay in Women's Surgical described as such.

'When? Where?' he asked in the same tight tone.

'I'm not sure when, but it will be somewhere in the Midlands,' she explained, trying to stick to the truth as much as possible.

'That doesn't sound very exciting.'

'It's more often the company that makes a holiday than the location,' she said with a taut smile. She'd be willing to camp out in Piccadilly bus station for a week if *he* was her holiday companion.

'So you'll be spending it with someone special?'

She could answer that question truthfully enough. When surgery was needed there was no one who figured more importantly in one's life than the person who was going to perform it.

'Yes, you could say that.'

'Why did you go rushing off on Saturday night?' That was his next question.

'Safety in numbers, maybe?'

'So that was it, and you wonder why you're taken at face value all the time?'

'I'm not with you.'

'Come off it, Leonie,' he said angrily. 'Have you forgotten how we were before the others arrived?'

'No.'

'So why play the nervous virgin?'

'Because that's what I am!' she flared. 'And for reasons that might surprise you!'

The car park was filling up with staff arriving for duty, and when she saw Joanne and Jean approaching she departed, aware as she hurried on her way that her heart was thumping, her head was aching, and her spirits were at zero.

Whether it was due to the heated confrontation with Adam, or part and parcel of what she could expect these days, by the time she'd reached the paediatric unit Leonie was feeling decidedly unwell.

'You weren't ill yesterday, were you?' Simon asked when he saw her. 'Only you look ghastly.'

'No. I went to visit a friend,' she told him faintly, as the room seemed to tilt around her.

By the time it had righted itself Simon and Beth were waiting to start ward rounds. As they eyed her enquiringly, Leonie said, 'Start without me, will you? I'll catch you up in a moment.'

It was only twenty yards to the staff restaurant and she decided that a strong black coffee might put her back on track.

As she drooped over the table, with the steaming cup in front of her, she heard Adam's voice nearby in conversation with the man who was in charge of the hospital porters. She shrank down in the seat. It was less than fifteen minutes since she'd left him and she was already having a break.

It went without saying that he was going to see her, and as the two men came into view she lifted her head defiantly.

As he opened his mouth to speak Simon's voice came from behind her, telling her in what was supposed to be a whisper, but could be heard quite clearly by all who were nearby, that there was an emergency on the ward and could she come straight away?

If Adam's face had been closed against her at their earlier

meeting, now it was as cold as an arctic waste, and with a
bravado that she instantly regretted Leonie said casually,
'Hi, there. Just having a quick coffee.' Then she followed
Simon out of the restaurant.

CHAPTER NINE

'SORRY about that,' Leonie told Simon as they hurried back to the ward. 'I wasn't having a premature lunch-break. I felt faint.'

He looked at her in concern. 'Do you think you came back too soon?'

She shook her head. 'No. It's not that. I think it was the heat that got to me. It's so warm on the wards.'

It was an excuse but he accepted it, having no reason to think otherwise.

As she bent over the bed, where the child who was at the centre of the emergency was haemorrhaging from the mouth, everything else was forgotten in the urgency of the moment. The toddler had been admitted with Christmas disease, a similar fault in blood clotting to that of haemophilia and called after the first person to be diagnosed with it.

It was caused by the deficiency in the blood of a protein called Factor IX, while in haemophilia the lack of Factor VIII created the problem.

A visiting relative had given the child a whistle to play with and when it had fallen over in its cot with the toy in its mouth, the whistle had gouged into the soft membrane of the roof and caused severe bleeding.

As Leonie was preparing to give an infusion of the missing factor to check the haemorrhaging, Adam came into the ward in the company of a pleasant, middle-aged woman who was the part-time teacher appointed by the education authority to provide some degree of schooling for long-stay children.

'I intend to get on to the department concerned,' he was saying to his companion. 'The need for schooling here comes only second to health care. Any cutbacks will not be acceptable. We have spent a considerable sum on providing an attractive classroom environment and want to see it made use of to the full.'

He was speaking forcefully but with his gaze fixed thoughtfully on her, and Leonie wondered just what was going through his mind.

There was no way that Adam would intrude when she was with a patient. If he did have something to say about the episode in the restaurant it would come later.

As the teacher continued on her way, rounding up her small pupils as she went, Derek came into the ward. As he and Adam chatted Leonie had the feeling that their eyes were on her, that their low-voiced conversation concerned her.

You're getting paranoid, she told herself as she treated the sick child. They'll have more important things to discuss than your affairs.

Derek might have, but what about Adam? He was on her case. Watchful and puzzled, he wasn't letting anything she did escape him.

If Leonie had been early with her morning coffee, her lunch-break didn't materialise until mid-afternoon due to a prolonged meeting of medical staff and administrative personnel with regard to the procedure and facilities available—or otherwise—when emergencies requiring extra beds and staff occurred.

Adam was in the chair as the functions they were discussing came under his jurisdiction.

'You may recall that not long ago we had a school bus crash to deal with and had to cope with a sudden influx of injured teenagers,' he was saying as she slid into a seat at the back of the room, having only just been able to get away from the ward.

'Accident and Emergency, along with our paediatric unit, controlled the situation with speed and efficiency, and at the time I was satisfied that our resources were sufficient to deal with this kind of emergency. But complacency and achievement are uneasy bedfellows, which is why I've called this meeting today to see if we can improve our responses when this kind of thing occurs.

'Is there anything we can learn from such a crisis? Obviously, sufficient staff and available beds must be our first priority, but what about theatre facilities? Do we have enough? And what about the standard of communication between ourselves and the paramedics?'

There was silence for a moment and then everyone seemed to be speaking at once, with the exception of herself, and she thought that if Adam saw that as a further display of disinterest in what was going on around her, he was welcome to do so.

The truth of the matter was that she had enough to cope with at the moment without being expected to produce pearls of wisdom on the running of the hospital. Also, knowing him, he would already have set the wheels in motion if the introduction of further improvements was feasible.

He held up his hand for silence, and as the babble of chatter subsided he proceeded to give substance to that surmise.

'Some of us have long thought that another theatre would be an enormous asset to our work here, and at a recent meeting of The Friends of St Mark's it was suggested that they instigate a drive to raise funds for that purpose.

'Obviously, it will take a lot of time and effort but, as we are all aware, when The Friends decide to do something they waste no time. If any of you are approached to assist with their fund-raising—in any way at all—I hope that you'll give them every co-operation.'

The announcement of the possibility of such an improvement to the hospital's facilities brought forth a spate of questions that all needed answers, and by the time the meeting broke up it was well into the afternoon.

'I'm afraid we're all going to be rather late for lunch. The meeting did go on longer than I intended,' Adam's voice said from behind her as Leonie left the discussion.

'Er...yes, it did,' she said quietly, without meeting his eyes.

'Are you hungry?' he asked.

'Yes. I'm starving. Why do you ask?'

'No reason.'

'So you're not checking up on how long it is since my last visit to the restaurant?' she challenged lightly.

His face became blank. 'Why? Should I be? If you really want to know, I was about to suggest that you join me at my usual eating place across the Irwell bridge.' He sighed. 'Though God knows why. Every time we're in each other's company I feel that I understand you less.

'You're a good doctor, one of the best, but in your work here, as in your life away from this place, I feel that you're holding something back. Your personal affairs are your own concern, but your approach to St Mark's is mine, so do get with it, eh, Leonie?'

She felt the blood rush to her cheeks and words of protest sprang to her lips, but what was there to protest about? Adam was right. She *was* holding something back. Whether in wisdom or stupidity she didn't know, but after that slap on the wrist there was no way she could force down her lunch seated across from him.

'Thanks for the invitation to join you,' she said with an attempt at calmness, 'but after the doubts you've just

voiced I think I'll give it a miss and eat with those who
aren't so unsure of me.'

'Suit yourself,' he told her levelly. 'It wasn't a good idea,
anyway.'

As he strode off, the longing to run after him, throw
herself into his arms and gasp out the truth was so strong
she felt faint again, but her senses steadied as the sane part
of her mind took over.

You could leave St Mark's, her little voice said. It isn't
the only hospital in the country. Seeing Adam all the time
is making it harder. You won't ever get him out of your
system but at least you can remove him from your orbit.
He was contented enough before you came along so don't
flatter yourself that he'll pine away when you've gone.

As Adam crossed the small wooden bridge that spanned
the Irwell his face was bleak. Why did he keep persisting
with Leonie? he asked himself. She was a Jekyll-and-Hyde
character. One moment she was bright, uncomplicated,
hard-working, and the next she was more of an onlooker
than a participant—and it was that side of her that he had
deep reservations about.

Derek felt the same—that her enthusiasm for the job
came and went. But he was only concerned from an efficiency point of view. The old fellow didn't have the beautiful blonde doctor in his mind all the time for other reasons.

Maybe Joanne could throw some light on the mystery,
if mystery it was. There was no one more forthright than
she, and she'd known Leonie for a long time. He would
speak to her at the first opportunity, and if he made a complete fool of himself by doing so he would just have to grin
and bear it.

Strangely, when he called her into his office she wasn't

as forthcoming as he'd expected, which perturbed him even more.

'If there's something Leonie is keeping back, it's up to her to tell you,' she said evasively when he asked if there was anything he ought to know about her friend. 'All I can say is that she's completely honourable. If there is something in her life that could affect the job or…' she paused and Adam sensed that she was choosing her words '…a personal relationship, you can rely on it not being anything that she is to blame for.'

He found himself frowning irritably. 'Well, thanks for that. You've been a great help. I'm now even more confused than before.'

'Don't be, Adam,' she said earnestly. 'When I tell her how concerned you are she'll realise that you need to talk.'

He shook his head. 'We did that earlier today and it got us exactly nowhere.'

'Hmm. Well, maybe when I've had a word the next time won't be like that.'

'I wouldn't like to bet on it,' he growled, and as she went back to her duties the only thing clear in his mind was the thought that Joanne knew something and she wasn't saying.

'Adam is on the warpath,' Joanne said when she rang Leonie later that night. 'He's been asking me if I know what ails you.'

'And?' Leonie asked quickly.

'And, of course, I didn't tell him.'

'Thank goodness for that,' Leonie breathed. 'If one day he has to know, I want to be the one who imparts the glad tidings.'

'You're not being fair to him,' Joanne protested. 'He's kind and decent and—'

'Those are two of the reasons I can't bring myself to tell him,' Leonie broke in. 'He might take me on out of pity.'

'Rubbish!' her friend declared. 'All men don't see us as breeding machines. In fact, these days they think twice before rushing into fatherhood.'

'And you think that Adam is like that?' Leonie asked quietly.

'Er, no, I don't,' Joanne had to admit. 'I've seen the way he is with my two.'

'There you are, then. I rest my case.'

'But, Leonie, how are you going to get round being away for the operation?'

'I've already paved the way. Adam thinks I'm going on holiday in the Midlands with a very special friend.'

'You're crazy! Catch me doing that if a gorgeous man was panting for me.'

'Yes, well, you haven't got my problem, have you?'

'No. I haven't,' Joanne agreed on a more serious note. 'If I had, maybe I would feel the same as you.'

During the days that followed Leonie was aware of increasing tiredness and breathing discomfort, but she managed to conceal it. Or, rather, she thought she had until Joanne remarked one morning that she looked like a washed-out ghost.

'How much longer is it going to be before the Birmingham people send for you?' she asked as Leonie paused in her stride along the hospital's main corridor.

'Any day, I should imagine,' she said with a pale smile.

'Hasn't Adam said anything about it?'

'About what?'

'About your general appearance.'

'He's given up on me. Doesn't even look the side I'm on these days.'

'That's not true!' Joanne exclaimed. 'I caught him look-

ing at you in the dining room the other day, but then
Amanda appeared and he switched his attention to her.
Thank goodness there's something for him to be happy
about. Those two have been given a new lease of life since
finding each other.'

'Yes,' she agreed, and thought that was what she desperately needed—a new lease of life. But what sort of a
life would it be without him?

Joanne changed the subject.

'What about the sports day on Saturday in the hospital
grounds? Do you think you'll be going? *We* intend to be
there—me, the girls and Phil, and Mum says that she might
come if she feels up to it.'

'I don't know,' Leonie said slowly. 'I've nothing else
planned. I'll have to think about it.'

She wasn't going to tell her friend that she spent every
moment away from St Mark's slumped on the sofa like a
limp rag doll.

The sports day was the first fund-raising event that The
Friends of St Mark's had arranged towards the new operating theatre, and Adam had asked that they support whatever was organised to that end.

As if reading her mind, Joanne informed her, 'Adam is
organising the events. I've been roped in for the hundred
metres and the tug-o-war and I'm helping in the teatent.
I'm surprised he hasn't tried to get you involved.'

Leonie swallowed hard. To get there at all would take
enough effort without any other drains on her energy. She
wasn't going to complain if she was overlooked.

She should have known better. He collared her one
morning as she was making her way to the wards, and at
the sound of his voice Leonie breathed a silent prayer of
thanks.

For once she was feeling all right. There was colour in
her cheeks and a spring in her step. How long it would last

was another matter, but for the moment—this moment when Adam was seeking her out—she was relieved that it was so.

'About Saturday,' he said easily, without any formal greeting. 'I'm short of contestants and helpers in the various functions. Maybe you'd like to volunteer?'

Her pleasure at being in his company was diminishing. He'd sought her out to fill in the gaps.

'How do you know that I intend being there?'

Rolling his eyes heavenwards, he tutted. 'I might have known! Don't you remember me asking for staff to give their support to any fund-raising efforts that came along?'

'Yes, I do, but that doesn't mean that you control what we do in our spare time, does it?' she pointed out with sweet reason.

'What is it with you, Leonie?' he protested. 'You won't put yourself out for anybody, will you?'

'Maybe you'd explain what you want me to do?'

He was turning away but that brought him swivelling back to face her. 'Got through to your conscience, have I?'

'Just tell me what you want me to do,' she insisted woodenly, with a feeling that she was making the nails for her own coffin—in more ways than one.

'Long jump, hundred metres, relay races? Opening the proceedings?'

She was goggling at him. 'What?'

'There will be myself and the chairman of the trust on the platform, but we also thought of having a runner with an imitation Olympic torch appearing at the start of the event. You have all the attributes for such a role, grace, style—and long legs.'

And a wheezy chest, pale face and a lethargy second only to sleeping sickness, she thought grimly.

'I don't think I'd be suitable for such a part,' she said stiffly, 'but—'

'Here we go again!' he grated. 'Forget it! I'll find someone else.'

He started to leave again but she put out a hand to restrain him.

'But, I was about to say, I'll do my best…and you can
put me into whatever events you like as long as it doesn't
include tossing the caber or wrestling.'

That brought forth a wintry smile.

'I'll bear that in mind. And I can rely on you for the rest
of it?'

'Yes, you can rely on me,' she said heavily. If she died
in the attempt they'd be able to put on her grave that she
could be relied on.

'I must go,' she said quickly as the hands of the clock
above them indicated that she should already be on duty,
'or there'll be yet another black mark against me.'

'Refer them to me if there is,' he called after her but she
was already out of sight.

Saturday dawned warm and sunny, and as Leonie drew
back the bedroom curtains there would have been pleasure
inside her at the thought of the day ahead if only she hadn't
been involved in the sports day. But she was, because she
couldn't bear to be any lower in Adam's esteem than she
was already.

In the first few moments after waking she felt reasonably
well, which wasn't unusual after a night's rest, but it was
how she would feel later in the day that was bothering her.

Joanne had been both pleased and concerned when she'd
learned that Adam had coerced her into taking part in the
afternoon's events.

'You'll look gorgeous as you come sprinting in with the
torch,' she'd said, 'but are you up to it—and the events
he's put you down for afterwards?'

'I'll have to be, won't I?' Leonie had said. 'I'm sick of being treated as a passenger.'

'They don't see you like that on the wards,' Joanne had protested. 'Beth and her staff and Simon think you're the bee's knees…and the kids adore you.'

Leonie had felt a lump come into her throat. That should have been all that mattered. What Adam and Derek thought could have gone by the board as long as she'd fulfilled her commitments to the children in her care.

And now the day of her ordeal had arrived. If she'd been feeling well she'd have thoroughly enjoyed the thought of helping the hospital…and being with Adam in the process.

But at least if she got through it without making a fool of herself it would be something to remember if she did leave St Mark's, which at the time seemed the sensible thing to do.

Maybe one day she might meet a man who already had a family and didn't want any more children, who wouldn't see her as faulty goods. If she was denying Adam the chance to make a decision on that score, it wasn't with spite or ill intent. It was because she loved him desperately.

The hospital lawns where the sports day was to be held sloped down to the banks of the Irwell, and the previous day Adam had informed her in more cordial tones than at their previous meeting that she was required to make her appearance running along the river bank, holding the torch high aloft.

'What are you intending to wear?' he'd wanted to know.

'Don't tell me I'm allowed to decide something for myself!' she'd exclaimed in mock astonishment.

A smile had hovered briefly.

'That depends on what it is.'

'A matching pale blue vest and shorts, and trainers on my feet?'

'Fine. You read my thoughts exactly. I wish it was a reciprocal procedure.'

'I don't want to argue with you any more, Adam,' she'd said with cool pleasantness. 'I'm doing this for St Mark's. That it happens to meet with your approval is a bonus.'

As Leonie ran along the river bank, with the torch held aloft, the crowd on the hospital lawns came into view, creating a bright splash of colour beneath the summer sun.

A cheer went up when they saw her, but at that moment Leonie felt her chest tighten. 'Not now,' she groaned. 'Please, not now!'

Her breathing became easier and the tension left her. If there was one day when she wanted to appear fit and well it was today. Just for once she wanted to enjoy herself without the dread of what might be hovering over her.

With her hair free of its plaits the long golden swathe streamed out behind her as she veered towards the waiting spectators.

Behind them she could see Adam and Mary Challenor seated on a small wooden platform. Beside it was a tall urn that someone had rooted out for the occasion, waiting for her to deposit the torch in it as an indication that the games had begun.

She was gasping for breath now, but no one was going to question that as she'd just done a longish run. When she flashed Adam a triumphant smile he saluted her with the warmth that had been missing for so long. So far, so good, she thought.

The rest of the afternoon wasn't so trouble-free. As Leonie took part in the events Adam had put her down for, coming way behind in all of them, she was conscious of his eyes on her full of brooding questions.

When it came to the last two races she backed out, telling the head of Pathology, who was in charge, that she'd sprained her ankle. When he nodded understandingly she limped off, hoping that she was making a convincing exit.

Behind a clump of bushes she lay on the grass with her eyes closed, her chest heaving and her heart thumping. She'd done what Adam had wanted, except for the last couple of races, and even for him she wasn't prepared to kill herself.

As soon as she got her breath back she was going to leave. A discreet departure was called for.

'I believe you've hurt your ankle,' Adam's voice said suddenly from above, and when she looked up he was outlined against a cobalt sky.

'Er, yes, I have,' she mumbled.

He bent down beside her. 'Which one?'

'The left,' she said, sliding it out of his reach.

'Let me see,' he commanded, and before she could object he was examining her foot with gentle fingers.

'Where does it hurt?' he asked as she squirmed uneasily at his touch.

'Difficult to say.'

'Surely you know where the pain is—if there is any.' His concern was turning to disapproval. 'Or was it an excuse to get away—back to doing the things you prefer to do?'

Leonie struggled to her feet and eyed him stonily.

'Yes, it was. Are you satisfied? Why should I spend the afternoon running round like an idiot to please you?'

'You weren't supposed to be doing it to please me,' he snapped. 'You were meant to be helping to raise funds for the hospital where we are both employed. I thought for a moment I'd misjudged you, but I should have known better.'

'And now that you've got my measure, what are you going to do about it?' she challenged. 'Because you can't fault my work, and what I do with the rest of my life is my business.'

What his reply to that question might have been she didn't find out. Amanda was approaching with the special smile on her face that she reserved for Adam, and Leonie ached with envy.

If *she* had been his sister, there would have been no problem. She could have told him about the spherocytosis without any hesitation. But it wasn't that easy, and with a casual wave in Amanda's direction she went to say good-bye to Joanne and her family, before making her solitary way home.

After Saturday's events Sunday dragged by, boring and empty, a void to be got through, but a welcome respite nevertheless before Monday morning.

Each time Leonie looked at the phone she willed it to ring, for Adam's voice to be at the other end, advocating peace instead of war. But it was late evening before it rang and when the call came it was from an unexpected source.

The husky tones coming over the line belonged to Amanda, and when she heard what Adam's sister had to say her face became blank with shock.

There had been a fire on one of the houseboats at the marina late on Saturday night. Two teenagers had been left to their own devices for the weekend by their parents, and a forgotten cigarette had set fire to upholstery in the cabin while the youngsters had been asleep.

At risk from fumes as much as the actual fire, they had been rescued in the nick of time before the boat had gone up in flames...and by whom?

'All the other boat-owners were out. Adam was the only one around, and needless to say, when he saw what was happening he went on board to get them out,' Amanda told her raggedly.

'They're safe, but all three are in St Mark's, suffering from smoke inhalation and superficial burns. I thought you'd want to know.'

'How bad are they?' she asked frantically.

'The teenagers were semi-conscious when he brought them out but they came round after a few moments. Adam is the worst affected as he went back into the smoke, believing there was another kid on board. He'd seen three of them on deck earlier, but it turned out that the friend had gone.'

'I can be there in ten minutes,' Leonie told her. 'Are you at the hospital now?'

'Yes. But I'm going home shortly as I've been here most of the day so you can have him to yourself, but I must warn you that he's not in the best of moods. To begin with, he's fuming that the young folk could have been so careless, angry that his beloved *Apple* was put at risk and totally fed up that he's ended up on the other side of the sheets in St Mark's. But I'm sure he'll cheer up when he sees you, Leonie, even though he did insist that you shouldn't be told.'

So the hero of the hour wasn't basking in glory? she thought grimly as she got the car out. But, then, he wouldn't be, would he? Adam wasn't one for fuss. Efficiency was what he got a buzz from, and the previous night's incident had been created through rank carelessness.

Why had he wanted her kept out of it? she wondered. The man was crazy. If she hadn't found out today, she would have discovered what had happened tomorrow when she turned up for work.

Maybe it was his way of making it even more clear that she was out of his life, that what happened to him wasn't her concern. If that were so, it was just too bad as she couldn't wait to get to him.

He could have died in the fire, and if he had she would

have wanted to die, too. Was this the answer she'd been seeking? That as long as they had each other, nothing else mattered?

But it didn't change anything, did it? She still couldn't give the man she loved healthy children. There was no greater sense of failure than that.

Adam was lying disconsolately in a small private ward, with dressings on his right hand, forehead and the side of his neck. There was oxygen equipment nearby that told the story of the previous night's events, and Leonie's heart skipped a beat at the thought of how much worse it could have been.

When she appeared at the side of his bed she saw pleasure on his face for a fleeting moment, then he croaked in a voice that was a far cry from his usual brisk tones, 'What are *you* doing here, Leonie?'

Resisting the urge to tell him that she was there because she loved him, she said lightly, 'I'm here to check that you're no worse than Amanda described.'

'So it was she who told you I was here. I gave her strict instructions that—'

'I wasn't to be told you'd nearly died, rescuing your neighbour's children? Why, for heaven's sake? Are you so averse to me that I'm to be kept out of something like this? Didn't you know that I'd be frantic to hear that you'd risked your life in such a manner?'

He sighed. 'It was because I didn't want to cause you distress that I instructed that you shouldn't be informed...but, in any case, what are *my* affairs to you? You're a mystery to me, Leonie. You're like mist—swirling, beckoning, but most of all concealing, and I can't deal with that. I have to be able to see where I'm going.'

'I didn't come here for another lecture on my shortcomings,' she said without raising her voice. 'I came because I care, believe it or not, and I'm devastated that it was hours after the event before I was told what had happened to you.'

'So it really does matter…what happens to me?' he breathed, taking her smooth, ringless hand in his. 'The shutters are finally gone? We can start making progress?'

It wasn't quite as simple as that, she thought guiltily, but at that moment, observing the dressings on his burns and listening to the hoarseness of his voice, in her relief she would have promised him the moon.

She was spared from making any commitments that she mightn't be able to keep when a reprieve in the form of the night sister appeared at that moment.

'I'm going to have to ask you to leave, Dr Marsden,' she said tactfully. 'Mr Lockhart still has some breathing difficulty and should be talking as little as possible.'

'I understand,' she told the nurse. 'I'll be on my way.'

When the sister had gone Adam said, 'If they don't discharge me tomorrow I shall be working from this room.' His voice softened. 'So you'll know where to find me.'

She nodded, her eyes tender, her heart aching with love for him. 'I'll bear that in mind… And now I must go before I'm thrown out. Just one more thing, though.'

'What?'

'*The Apple*. Is it damaged at all? Do you want me to go there to check it out?'

Adam shook his head. 'No. The boat is all right. The fire was extinguished before it spread to other craft. Amanda has made sure that it's safe and secure so you have no need to concern yourself.'

'Fine. I'll be off, then.'

Bending, she put her arms around him and for a brief moment, with her lips against his hair, she held him close.

'Until tomorrow, Adam,' she said gently.

As her arms fell away he reached out for her, but she shook her head. 'You heard what the sister said.'

He was laughing up at her. 'I only heard what you had

to say and that was Dr Marsden's lightning cure for burns and boredom. You won't get away so easily tomorrow.'

'That's something to look forward to, then,' she said lightly, tuning into his mood.

'Do you mean that?'

'Of course I do,' she said gently, and as the sister began to hover again she left.

CHAPTER TEN

WHEN Leonie arrived at St Mark's on Monday morning she went straight to Adam's room, before presenting herself in the clinic or on the wards.

She couldn't wait to be with him—to speak to him, touch him, see with her own eyes that he was making a satisfactory recovery—but her step faltered as she approached the open door of the small side ward.

It sounded as if the room was full of people, and when she cast a quick look inside she could see that it was so. A doctor was bending over him with a nurse hovering. Jean was seated behind her computer at a small desk that hadn't been there the night before.

Mary Challenor had also put in an appearance, which had to be some measure of her regard for him as it was unheard of for the head of the trust to be in the hospital at such an hour.

She was chatting to Amanda, who must have had the same idea as Leonie herself—to see Adam before the day got under way.

The atmosphere in the room seemed relaxed enough. They obviously weren't there because of a worsening of his condition. It was simply a gathering of the clans. Feeling surplus to requirements, she made a quick departure before she was observed.

As she arrived on the ward a child was being admitted with suspected kidney problems. Two-year-old Jessica had been seen by her GP because of pallor and listlessness. According to her parents, she'd had a swollen face every morning during the last week and their anxiety had been increasing daily.

On discovering that there was a large amount of fluid in the tissues and much protein in the child's urine, the family doctor had requested admission to hospital for further tests, and now here she was, a pale-faced toddler with big problems.

From previous experience of children with similar symptoms Leonie knew that a low-salt diet would be required and diuretic drugs prescribed to combat the excess fluid if tests showed that it was indeed damage to the filtering units of the kidneys that they were going to have to deal with. Oral prednisolone was also one of the medications given in such cases, with a gradual reduction of the steroid as the condition improved.

While she was examining little Jessica another patient was wheeled in from Casualty, and Leonie was dismayed to see that Jacob Motassi was back.

He had been admitted with severe pain in the lower spine and vomiting, and once the nurses had settled him into the one vacant bed Leonie took over.

Although Jacob's type of haemolytic anaemia was different from her own, the sight of the suffering teenager was enough to remind her that her brief happiness of yesterday might only be a fleeting thing.

But as she looked down at the face that was twisted with pain, her own affairs receded into second place. This was Jacob's second infarctive crisis in as many months and it was worrying.

She immediately arranged for intravenous fluids to be given to combat dehydration and morphine for pain relief, with instructions to Beth that she was to be informed immediately if the boy showed any signs of worsening.

The day wasn't going well. It had started off on the wrong foot, with Adam's room being like Piccadilly Circus in the rush hour, and now the children's ward was full, with a sick child in every bed.

This wasn't an unusual occurrence but, for some reason, today it depressed her more than usual. However, the most disturbing event had yet to come.

It was half past eleven and for the first time she was free to go to see Adam, but as she was about to leave the ward the phone rang and Beth called from the office, 'It's for you, Dr Marsden.'

Leonie sighed. Was she never going to get away? When she heard the voice at the other end of the line any urgency to be with Adam went.

It was James, and after they'd exchanged greetings he said, 'How are you, Leonie?'

'I'm struggling, James,' she said wryly. 'Lack of energy, breathlessness and the rest.'

'What would you say if I told you that one of the surgeons here has a vacant slot tomorrow and he's willing to do your op? As it's classed as non-urgent I haven't been able to rush it through for you, and if you don't take this offer it could be weeks before he can fit you in again. What do you say?'

'I don't know whether I can get the time off at such short notice,' she said shakily, as all the implications sank in. 'I have my commitment here to consider. Also, Adam is hospitalised at the moment. He was involved in rescuing some young people from a fire and is being kept in St Mark's for the time being.'

'He's not seriously hurt, is he?' James asked.

'No, but I'd like to be here for him in case he needs me.'

'And do you think he would want you to postpone something as important as this on his behalf?' he asked. 'Go for it, Leonie. In spite of what I said at the beginning, I know that I'll be happier when your spleen has been removed. Your general health will improve immensely.'

'And the health of any children I might have?'

'That I can't make any promises about, as you well know, but it certainly isn't reason to shilly-shally about the operation. We're talking about your health—your life even—and it can only improve the quality of it. I'm sure that Lockhart wouldn't begrudge you that. I'll give you until lunchtime. Ring me then and let me know what you've decided.'

'Yes, all right, I'll do that,' she agreed sombrely. As the line went dead she stood gazing at the receiver in her hand as if it might have the answer.

'Do as James advises,' Joanne said when Leonie told her about his phone call. 'Your only alternative would be to have the operation performed here, where you would probably get more priority, but you don't want to do that, do you?'

Leonie shook her head. 'No. I want to be away from Adam when it's done. If I was operated on here he would be in on it and I don't want that.'

Her friend looked at her sympathetically. 'I know you don't and I can understand why, but only up to a point. You're behaving as if the spherocytosis turns you into some kind of leper. Don't you think you're letting the implications of it get out of hand?'

'Maybe,' Leonie conceded gloomily, 'but I can't help the way I feel. Getting back to what James had to say, how can I ask for time off at such short notice under the guise of wanting to take a holiday? And, even worse, leave Adam when he's hospitalised?'

'That's the last thing he'll be bothered about, having you there to smooth his fevered brow. Knowing him, he'll be champing at the bit to get into harness again.

'It's the fact that you're buzzing off just as he thinks everything is right between you again that will get to him and, even worse, that you're dumping his beloved hospital with only hours to spare. That is, of course, providing you can get leave.'

Leonie groaned. 'Thanks for the words of comfort. I feel even more depressed now.'

'Your first move should be to see how difficult it's going to be to get the time off,' Joanne went on. 'If the paediatric unit can get a replacement or a locum at short notice, that's your first hurdle crossed. No sense in worrying about the second yet. On that point I wouldn't go to visit Adam until you see how the land lies with the other doctors. Keep your fingers crossed that none of them have booked the same dates.'

Leonie nodded. 'Yes. I will. I'll go and sound them out now.'

'It's extremely short notice,' Derek said tetchily when she asked if it would be convenient for her to take a couple of weeks off. 'I have nothing planned myself,' he went on in the same snappy tone, 'but young Harris might have, or my assistant, Paul Conway, could be due for time off.'

'I've checked with the rest of the staff and it's all right with them,' Leonie said uncomfortably.

'Is it? Well, it isn't all right with me, having a doctor short. And it won't be all right with Adam Lockhart, unless he can get a replacement for you. It is most inconvenient, but I have noticed, Dr Marsden, that most of the time your own affairs seem to take precedence over your commitment to St Mark's.'

She wanted to cry, Yes, but as well as belonging to the medical profession, I'm also one of the sick and suffering, and for that reason might be forgiven for being somewhat preoccupied with myself.

Instead, she said meekly, 'I'm sorry that you think that of me, sir, but I can assure you that I wouldn't be making this request if it weren't very important.'

The elderly paediatric surgeon cleared his throat irritably. 'That's all very well, but Adam Lockhart will have the last word. I'm going to visit him now on another matter and I'll see what he has to say.'

Leonie turned away. If Derek had been more accommodating there would have been no need for Adam to know until she'd gone. In situations like this the doctors sorted it out amongst themselves, covering for each other.

The clinical services manager was only involved when there was likely to be a staffing problem, and she supposed in fairness that this could be one of those occasions. But for Adam to find out that she was doing a disappearing act just as they were back on a friendly footing, would put the death knell on their relationship.

But if he didn't find out today he would get to know tomorrow, and so, when Jean called from the private ward where they were working to say that he wanted to see her, Leonie braced herself for what was to come.

When she got there he was alone, whether by accident or design she didn't know.

'I thought you couldn't wait to see me today,' he greeted her coolly, 'but as it's almost lunchtime it would appear that the urgency has disappeared, which is perhaps connected with what Derek has just been telling me.'

'I came by before eight o'clock this morning,' she said quietly, 'but there was no point in me staying as it was full of people.'

'And since?'

'I've been dealing with two new admissions...and talking to Derek, as you have discovered.'

Adam looked tired and disgruntled and oddly out of place, holding court from his hospital bed.

'I need to know how you are, Adam,' she said. 'I couldn't sleep for thinking about you.'

His smile was grim. 'You mean that you don't want to

go on this sudden holiday of yours if there's any chance
that I might have a relapse and add to your sense of guilt.'

'No, I don't,' she said steadily. 'And how do you know
I feel guilty?'

'I don't. But I was hoping that you might. It would make
me feel less angry at the way you're deserting me. You
said last night that you cared. What a lie that was!'

'It was the truth,' she protested. 'I do.'

'So the phone call you had earlier from some man friend
has nothing to do with you suddenly wanting to see the
back of myself and St Mark's with all speed?'

'No! It's not like that. I can't deny that it has a lot to do
with it, but not in the way you think, Adam.'

'And how am I supposed to think? You're selfish and
devious, Leonie. Go on your holiday. I'll find a replacement
and if you decide not to come back there won't be any
tears shed.'

Except mine, she thought, as with a last long look she
left him.

'It's on,' she told James flatly when she phoned him in
her lunch-hour. 'My name is mud here, but what's new
about that?'

'They'll be pleased in the long run,' he said comfort-
ingly. 'A healthy doctor contributes more than an unhealthy
one.'

'Yes, I know,' she admitted in the same downbeat tone,
'but I can't get rid of the feeling that I'm handling it all
wrong.'

'Don't worry about anything like that for the moment,'
he advised. 'Just concentrate on getting here and being
ready for tomorrow. Can you come this evening?'

'Yes. I'll pack a bag when I get home and drive straight
to Birmingham.'

'Good... And, Leonie, it's only two weeks of your life

we're talking about. St Mark's isn't going to fold up just because you're missing.'

'I know that,' she told him wearily, 'but have you any idea what it's like to be as unpopular as I am?'

'When it's all over you can take up with Adam Lockhart where you left off,' he soothed.

'What? You mean at each other's throats?'

'He's insane if he doesn't want you.'

'Oh, I think he wants me all right, but as what he thinks I am, not as a half-woman.' On that dismal note she bade him goodbye.

While Leonie was driving to Birmingham Adam was on his way home to *The Apple*. He was still hoarse but his chest and lungs were clear and those treating him had felt that the lowness of spirit he was experiencing would disperse more quickly in his home surroundings.

They couldn't have known that his sombre mien had been due to the departure of Leonie to he knew not where and with whom, but Joanne had known the reason and she'd sought him out before making her way home at the end of the day.

'Thought I'd pop in to see the injured hero before I left,' she said breezily to the tall figure standing in sober thought by the ward window.

'Lay off it, Joanne,' he growled. 'You're too cheerful.'

'And you, my dear Adam, can't see any further than the end of your nose.'

'And what do you mean by that?' he snapped.

She wished she could have told him, but a promise was a promise.

'Think about it,' she suggested, making for the door as the thought occurred that the longer she stayed, the more likely she was to spill the beans.

'Are you talking about Leonie?' he asked, his dark eyes keen and watchful.

'Could be,' she admitted. 'But I must go—my family awaits me.'

'Who is she going on holiday with?' he persisted.

'Er...no one, as far as I know.'

'But she's meeting someone?'

'She's meeting a group of people.'

His face lightened. 'So it's not a one-to-one set-up?'

'No. Not exactly.'

'For God's sake, Joanne, put me out of my misery!' he bellowed.

'Only Leonie can do that.'

He nodded. 'I'm not going to argue about that. Has she left?'

'Half an hour ago. She went home to pack and then she was setting off...for her holiday.'

'A holiday in the Midlands,' he groaned. What could be so important about that?

He'd been away from *The Apple* for two days and normally would have been delighted to be back, but he wasn't. If his obsession with Leonie had made the boat lose its appeal, it would be the last straw.

But everywhere he looked he seemed to see her. How she'd appeared that first time when he'd caught her on the canal bank, looking over his home. How she'd been when, pale and ill, he'd brought her to *The Apple* wrapped in a blanket. Then there'd been the night of the dinner party when she'd been at her most beautiful in black and white.

All were images that made the life he'd been leading before he'd met her seem empty and meaningless. But why was he torturing himself?

She'd said once how she hated being taken at face value, but apparently that was all she was—an empty vessel that was beautiful on the outside, but with nothing behind the facade.

Joanne had hinted that he ought to know what was going on in Leonie's life. Well, he did. She was self-serving first, and those she encountered along the way were always a poor second, unless this fellow she was so desperate to join was the one she'd been seeking.

But as he tossed amongst the covers of his bed, other visions of her came to mind. Her care for the children who passed through Paediatrics. The way she'd looked after Rebecca and Tiffany when Joanne's mother had been ill. Leonie was kind and loving with them, so why couldn't she be like that with him, instead of being someone who always seemed to be saying one thing and meaning another?

On the few occasions when they'd found themselves in each other's arms it had seemed as if he'd come home after a long journey, and he would have sworn that she'd felt the same, but it had been wishful thinking—reaching for the moon and stars but never able to grasp them.

He sat up suddenly. She'd looked dreadful when they'd had their last fraught conversation. Supposing she was ill? He sank back against the pillows. Leonie was a doctor, for God's sake. If anyone ought to know they weren't well, she should. For the rest of the night his anger and confusion were replaced by concern, and he vowed that first thing in the morning Joanne was going to come clean, whether she wanted to or not.

James had been waiting when Leonie arrived at the large Birmingham hospital, and when she saw him smiling at her across Reception her eyes filled with tears.

'Hey,' he said gently. 'What's all this? No need to get upset. It's not a serious operation, you know. Just a matter of opening up the left side of your stomach and removing something that isn't a vital organ anyway. You shouldn't be in Theatre more than an hour.'

She managed a smile through her tears. 'Yes, I do know that, James. I'm crying because I've made a mess of everything. I've made myself unpopular on the unit back at St Mark's, and Adam thinks so badly of me I can hardly bear it.'

'Then send for him and tell him why you've been so secretive about what you're suffering from,' he suggested. 'You deserve to have the man you love with you at a time like this.'

She shook her head. 'No. I've come this far without telling him. Maybe afterwards…when I'm feeling better. Take me to the ward, James, and I'll settle myself in… And thanks for taking a slice out of your evening to meet me here.'

His long face broke into a smile. 'It was my pleasure and I'll be even more pleased tomorrow when the ordeal is over for you. The surgeon will be in to see you first thing in the morning. He'll tell you then what time he's going to operate.'

Twice during a night spent on stiff, starched sheets Leonie picked up the bedside phone to ring Adam, but on both occasions she resisted, telling herself that for one thing she didn't know if he'd gone home or was still at St Mark's, and, for another, would he want to be disturbed in the middle of the night while he was still recovering from the effects of the fire?

By morning she was feeling calmer. A visit from a couple of nurses she'd known when she'd been based there cheered her up, and it was comforting to be in familiar surroundings.

Feeling less isolated, she ignored the pangs of hunger, keeping her glance resolutely away from the NIL BY MOUTH sign above her bed, and prepared to face the day.

If she wasn't flavour of the month back at St Mark's with Adam and the paediatric team, at least she was doing something positive, instead of drooping around in a state of breathlessness and exhaustion all the time, she thought as the hands of the clock moved slowly round. She'd tried to pull her weight before, but after the splenectomy there'd be no touching her.

The surgeon had been and gone. Young and businesslike, he'd said with a smile, 'I believe you used to be in Paediatrics here. Why did you leave? I'm sure it must have been our loss.'

Her smile had been wistful around the edges. 'I was looking for further experience and moved to a bigger hospital.'

'And has it worked out?'

'Er, yes, I suppose so. I've been increasing my knowledge.'

'Good grief, Adam!' Joanne exclaimed when she opened the door at seven o'clock on Tuesday morning in answer to the insistent ring of the doorbell. 'Have you seen the time?'

'Yes, I have,' he said quickly. 'But we have to talk, Joanne.'

'What about?' she questioned warily.

'As if you didn't know.'

'Leonie?'

'Yes.'

She sighed. 'I've been thinking about her all night.'

'Why, when she's gallivanting off on holiday?'

Averting her glance from his, she said uncomfortably, 'Yes. Crazy, aren't I?'

'"Crafty" would be a better word,' he snapped. 'Stop treating me like a fool, will you, Joanne? She's ill, isn't she? Is that what the big mystery is about?'

It was a shot in the dark but he was desperate...and her jaw went slack with surprise.

'How did you guess?' she breathed, clutching her dressing-gown more tightly around herself as if its very fabric would protect her from the onslaught of his dark, accusing eyes.

'So I'm right. What's wrong with her? How serious is it? And where has she gone?'

He was firing the questions like bullets and Joanne slumped down onto the nearest chair. Could she tell him? Betray Leonie's confidence? There was more to it than just an illness.

'I can't tell you, Adam,' she said wretchedly. 'Not until I've spoken to her. I made her a promise that I wouldn't tell you and I can't break it.'

'So she could be dying, but you aren't going to put me in the picture,' he said harshly.

'It isn't as serious as that. It's the other implications of what's wrong with her that are creating the problem.'

'And you're not going to tell me, even though I love her desperately and can't exist without her. If she's ill I should be with her, not going quietly mad on the sidelines.'

Joanne eyed him compassionately. This busy man had given up his time to help look after her children in a crisis, as had the beautiful doctor he was agonising over. She loved them both dearly, and on a sudden impulse decided she could at least tell Adam half of what he wanted to know. The rest would be up to Leonie.

'I can tell you some of it, Adam,' she said sombrely. 'What is wrong and where she is—but the rest will be up to her.'

'Go on, then,' he commanded grimly.

Joanne could hear the children moving about upstairs and she prayed they wouldn't come dashing into this fraught moment. Because of that she found herself gabbling. 'Leonie has a form of haemolytic anaemia.'

'And?'

'She's gone to have a splenectomy to improve her general health, which has been somewhat on the decline of late.'

Adam's face was creased with amazed concern. 'And so why didn't she tell me?'

'That's the part of it that she'll have to want to tell you herself.'

'Are you informing me that she's been ill ever since joining St Mark's?'

'Yes. She'd had the tests before coming to Manchester and they phoned the results through from Birmingham on her first day in the new job.'

'And because of that she didn't want to be found wanting,' he said slowly. 'What a crazy, mixed-up woman.'

'She's had cause to be,' Joanne informed him, 'but that's all I'm prepared to say on the matter, except that she's gone to Birmingham to have the operation.'

'Rather than St Mark's?'

'Yes, for the same reasons she hasn't wanted to explain.'

'I see. Or rather I don't see, but I soon will. I'd intended going in to work for a few hours today but I'm going to give it a miss,' Adam said tightly. 'Tell my secretary that if she needs me for anything to try my home number tonight.'

'I take it that you're going to Birmingham?' Joanne said.

'You take it right, but first I'm going home to read up on…' He groaned. 'I can't, if you won't tell me the name of her illness.'

'Try spherocytosis,' she said as the lounge door opened to admit two small figures in cotton nighties. 'And the best of luck, Adam.'

Adam's first inclination was to fling himself in his car

and drive to where Leonie was, but common sense dictated that he needed to be prepared if there was something coming up that he might find hard to cope with.

As soon as he sat down on the boat deck with the *British Medical Encyclopedia* open at the appropriate page he knew why she had kept her illness from him.

When he'd finished reading he sat with bent head, alone in the quiet morning. There was sadness in him and when at last he got to his feet the impetus that had pulled at him before was missing.

Leonie was due to go to Theatre any second and as she waited she thought that today it was her turn to be on the other side of health care.

Adam had been the patient at the weekend and now she was to be the recipient of treatment. The only difference was that where he had been inundated with visitors, for her they would be few and far between...if any.

Obviously, James would stop by during her recovery but he was a busy man and she couldn't expect him to dance attendance on a casual acquaintance. So it would be a case of catching up on her reading...and her sleep.

The lack of visitors wasn't going to bother her. There was only one person she wanted by her side, and as he hadn't a clue where she was that wasn't going to happen.

If he did know, she doubted whether it would make much difference after their last chilly encounter because she'd let St Mark's down, and if he wasn't prepared to plead his own case he was fiercely protective of the hospital's needs.

A porter smiled down at her. The moment had come. 'Are you ready, lady?' he asked with a smile.

Leonie nodded. She was ready, and in that moment all other cares were cast aside to make way for the ordeal ahead.

*   *   *

When Adam got to the ward her bed was empty and his heart sank. The familiar NIL BY MOUTH sign above it told its own tale.

'Dr Mardsen is in Theatre,' a hovering nurse told him with a sympathetic glance at his dismayed face.

He nodded. 'Yes. How long before she gets back?'

'A couple of hours. She'll be taken to Recovery once the operation is over.'

He nodded again, this time impatiently. He knew the procedure, none better, but this young nurse wasn't to know that and he managed to dredge up a smile.

'Yes, of course. In the meantime, could you direct me to James Morgan's department?'

'Lockhart!' The haematologist's smile was welcoming enough but Adam saw that it didn't reach his eyes. They were wary, weighing him up to assess just how much he knew, and Adam thought bleakly that this man was the one Leonie had trusted in her predicament…not him.

'I take it that you're aware of what's going on?' James Morgan probed. 'Otherwise you wouldn't be here.'

'Yes. I am now aware of Leonie's illness,' Adam grated. 'I managed to persuade Joanne to tell me some of it and the *British Medical Encyclopedia* told me the rest. I've just discovered that she's being operated on at this moment. So, in the meantime, I'd like a few questions answered.'

'If I can,' the other man murmured.

'How long has Leonie had spherocytosis? As far as I'm aware, we at St Mark's have no record of it.'

'You wouldn't have. She had tests during her last weeks here and the results only came through, ironically enough, on her first day in your employ.'

That bore out what Joanne had told him. What a blight on her new job prospects, Adam thought grimly. No wonder she'd kept it quiet. But that hadn't been the main reason for secrecy, had it?

'The surgery at present taking place…she's not in any danger, is she?'

James shook his head. 'Not really. The splenectomy is to stop the spleen destroying the red blood cells faster than they can be produced. Her health should improve greatly once it's done.'

'So why wasn't it done before? Why wait all this time?'

'I'm partly to blame for that. As she was reasonably well at the time and desperate not to have to take time off, I suggested she leave it for a while.'

'But?'

'Recently she's been feeling far from well and so I advised that the operation should go ahead.'

'It sounds as if everyone knew except me!' Adam exclaimed grittily.

'Not really,' the haematologist said placatingly. 'Only three people knew. I did. So did her friend Joanne. And of course, Leonie herself. I imagine that you'll have worked out for yourself why she didn't want you to find out.'

'Yes, I have,' Adam admitted heavily. 'And as soon as she's well enough to talk we're going to sort this thing out.'

'That's what's needed,' he was told. 'I haven't been happy about you being kept in the dark as you mean an awful lot to her but, as we both know, there's such a thing as patient confidentiality.'

CHAPTER ELEVEN

As LEONIE gradually regained consciousness she was muzzily aware of a presence beside her, and as she lay with her eyes closed, getting to grips with the return to reality, she was silently thanking James for making the effort to be with her at such a moment.

But the voice that was gently saying her name was someone else's, and as she focused blearily on the face above her a solitary tear rolled down her cheek.

'Adam!' she breathed through parched lips. 'How did you...?'

'Know you were here?' he said with a smile.

'Mmm.'

'I gave Joanne the heavy treatment and she came up with half of the story. The medical encyclopaedia told me the rest, and I've had a revealing chat with your friend James Morgan.'

The tears were threatening again. 'So you know all about me, then?'

He took out a clean white handkerchief and wiped her wet cheeks. 'Yes, I do, but we'll talk about it later. If the nurses see that I'm upsetting you the moment you've come round from surgery I'll be out with a flea in my ear. I'll come back in a couple of hours.'

'You will?'

'I just said so, didn't I?'

'Mmmm.' She was drifting off again and with a hovering nurse about to eject him, he left, turning to look back over his shoulder before leaving the ward.

'So it's over,' Joanne said thankfully when he phoned her office at St Mark's.

'Yes, it's over,' he agreed flatly. 'All that remains now is to clear the air. But when I spoke to Leonie she'd only just come round from the anaesthetic. I'm going back to the ward shortly.'

'You're aware of the implications, then?' she said.

'Yes, I'm aware, and if you're going to ask me what I'm going to do, you'll have to wait and see.'

'Of course,' she agreed meekly, for once having no snappy answer. As they said their goodbyes she hoped that the sense of purpose in his voice boded well for her friend.

When Adam went back to the ward Leonie was sitting up, propped against the pillows in a blue nightdress the colour of her eyes.

Her hair hung limply on her shoulders, her face was pale and there were dark smudges beneath her eyes, but to the man striding towards her she had never been more beautiful.

'How are you feeling?' he asked the moment he reached her side.

She gave him a wan smile and trotted out the response that hospitals are prone to give in reply to an enquiry about a patient's health. 'As well as can be expected...under the circumstances.'

'And what circumstances might those be?' Adam asked gravely, taking her hand in his.

'The fact that I've just had an operation, for starters.'

'Anything else?'

'Don't pretend that you aren't aware of the rest of it, Adam,' she said wearily. 'Let's just get it over and done with.'

'What? That you might have children with the same problem as you?'

'Yes.'

'And because of that you think I won't want to know you?'

'You'd be crazy if you did.'

'Don't you think that *I* should be the judge of that, Leonie? I've just discovered that the woman I adore is prepared to bow out of my life because for some reason she sees this thing as a stigma. Is that right?'

'Yes, it is,' she mumbled.

'Well, let me tell you this. I find it amazing that you've taken it upon yourself to make this sort of decision without consulting me. For one thing, it's horrendous that you've carried this burden alone. I thought that when two people truly loved each other they shared everything—the good and the bad.

'I love children as much as the next man, but not to the extent that I'm going to marry someone I don't love to get them when the woman I care for has such a hold on my heart that I can't exist without her.'

Two bright spots of colour appeared on Leonie's pale cheeks as she listened to him. Was the nightmare she'd lived through during the last few months coming to an end?

'Haven't you heard of adoption, Leonie? Or fostering? Or the tests that could be possible on any babies we might make together? The patter of tiny feet could come from a few directions. And if none of those things work out, what does it matter as long as we've got each other?'

Tears were spilling down her cheeks. 'So you don't mind?'

'Of course I do. I mind like hell. But I know that any pain it causes me will be as nothing compared to the anguish that you'll have to deal with.

'So are we going to put all this behind us and look to the future?' he asked tenderly. 'Because even *The Apple* has lost its magic without you.'

'You really do want to marry me, then?' she asked in a voice that shook.

Adam laughed. 'Yes, I do, and if it weren't for the fact that you've recently had surgery I'd give you a demonstration of just how keen I am to do so, but I can wait, Leonie. I can wait for ever just as long as I know that you belong to me.'

It was her turn to laugh. 'I've been yours ever since I walked into a conference on a cold winter night and found the man I'd been looking for all my life. When I met you again at St Mark's I thought the fates were smiling on me, but they had something unpleasant up their sleeves, too, news of a complaint that was going to alter the whole course of my existence.'

'And what was that?' he asked guilelessly. 'Love?'

'Yes,' she said, her blue eyes dancing. 'Perhaps it would be more accurate to say I'm suffering from two incurable ailments, love...and spherocytosis.'

Leonie was back on the wards, happier than she'd ever been in her life—and healthier, too. As each day brought their wedding nearer, the man who loved her for what she was gave thanks for what he had.

Two small girls were looking forward to being bridesmaids at the ceremony in an old stone church not far from the marina, and James was deserting his busy haematology department in Birmingham to give Leonie away.

A delighted Joanne would be there with Phil, and Amanda and Roger were to be host and hostess at the reception in a smart waterfront restaurant.

However, for the moment it was business as usual, and as Leonie stopped by the bed of Jacob Motassi, who was only just beginning to show some improvement from his last attack of sickle-cell anaemia which had kept him hospitalised for weeks rather than days, she had a suggestion to make.

'How would you like to come to my wedding, Jacob?' she asked.

His huge eyes gazed up at her in surprise and then he smiled.

'You mean that, Doctor?'

'Yes, of course I do. We're friends, aren't we? And also, we've both got the same kind of illness.'

'Can I bring my drums?'

'Yes,' she told him laughingly. 'Just as long as you keep them for the reception. I don't want the organist to think he has competition.'

That evening, as Leonie stood with Adam's arms around her on the deck of *The Apple*, she told him that she'd invited Jacob to the wedding.

He eyed her quizzically. 'Why? There has to be a reason.'

'For one thing, I'm very fond of him,' she explained.

'And?'

'For another I'm constantly aware of how lucky I am. My illness is under control. I can live a normal life. For Jacob such a thing will never happen.'

'I thought that might be it,' Adam said gently. 'If it's going to be a count-your-blessings night, let's start from where we mean to go on.'

As his arms tightened around her slender, graceful body, and his mouth came down on hers, the gentle lapping of the water and the sway of the boat seemed to be saying the same thing that was in both their hearts…in Adam's small Eden all was well.

MILLS & BOON®

Makes any time special™

Mills & Boon publish 29 new titles every month. Select from...

Modern Romance™   **Tender Romance**™

Sensual Romance™

Medical Romance™   **Historical Romance**™

MAT2

For better, for worse... for ever
Brides and Grooms
Available at branches of WH Smith, Tesco, Martins, Borders, Easons,
Volume One/James Thin and most good paperback bookshops

FREE
4 BOOKS
AND A SURPRISE GIFT!

We would like to take this opportunity to thank you for reading this Mills & Boon® book by offering you the chance to take FOUR more specially selected titles from the Medical Romance™ series absolutely FREE! We're also making this offer to introduce you to the benefits of the Reader Service™ —

★ FREE home delivery
★ FREE gifts and competitions
★ FREE monthly Newsletter
★ Exclusive Reader Service discounts
★ Books available before they're in the shops

Accepting these FREE books and gift places you under no obligation to buy; you may cancel at any time, even after receiving your free shipment. Simply complete your details below and return the entire page to the address below. *You don't even need a stamp!*

YES! Please send me 4 free Medical Romance books and a surprise gift. I understand that unless you hear from me, I will receive 6 superb new titles every month for just £2.40 each, postage and packing free. I am under no obligation to purchase any books and may cancel my subscription at any time. The free books and gift will be mine to keep in any case.

MOZEC

Ms/Mrs/Miss/Mr ....Initials ....

BLOCK CAPITALS PLEASE

Surname ....

Address ....

....

....Postcode ....

Send this whole page to:
UK: FREEPOST CN81, Croydon, CR9 3WZ
EIRE: PO Box 4546, Kilcock, County Kildare (stamp required)

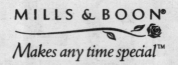